14
Steps

CAPPY HALL REARICK

DEDICATION

This book is dedicated to Elizabeth Utsey,
the mother-in-law every young bride should
be fortunate enough to know and love.

.

Books by Cappy Hall Rearick

Simply Southern

Simply Southern II

Simply Christmas

Simply Christmas II

Simply Southern Ease

Return to Rocky Bottom

Hey God, Let's Talk

50 Shades of Southern

The Road to Hell is Seldom Seen

High Cotton Christmas

I do! I do! I do!

Christmas Past

CONTENTS

About the Author

ACKNOWLEDGMENTS

In addition to the characters that pepper my books, I am indebted to my friends who encouraged me to keep on keeping on when I was more than ready to scrap every word, period and comma. No writer can claim sole responsibility for collecting words on paper that may or may not be read. Yes, we are the ones typing, proofing and editing and then doing it all over again the next day, but it is friends that make up our lives while we are making up our stories. They are as necessary to the writing process as computers, ink and copy paper. My amalgam of friends represent a world of loyalty and patience. They insist that I keep on writing when I am ready to chuck it all. They read my unfinished and unproofed manuscripts and make suggestions that I would never have thought of on my own. In short, they nag me to pieces. Becky Davis, Laverne Bardy, Mary Stripling, Amy Munnell, Sheila Hudson and Jan Kelleher make up some of my personal blessings especially when they nag. Through thick and thin these ladies had my back while writing this book and they still do. Thank you, my dear friends. I love you all.

Years ago when I began to write this book, Anne Salley told me about the contents she discovered once in an old trunk. Her thoughts became contributions to my story.

My husband Bill earns a few new stars in his crown with every book I write. My characters color and flavor my words but Bill Rearick seasons my life to make it taste more wonderful than I ever thought possible.

PROLOGUE

Bear River Falls, North Carolina 2015

Until recently, I lived and breathed one life and one life only.

Like a lot of people do, I hoard my share of secrets and hide from public scrutiny those things I choose to remain only mine until I decide otherwise. I am not by nature a furtive person but I became one the day I climbed 14 steps up to a neglected attic in search of an antique chair.

Instead of an old rocker there was an equally old humpback trunk placed there by my husband's mother before she died. In the days and weeks that followed, I was to discover that the trunk was filled with family history and keepsakes, all of which had been supplemented with hand-written letters of explanation.

At first the trunk's contents appeared to be ordinary things, the kind people save for posterity. In time I would come to realize and appreciate however, that it was the final resting place for the heart and soul of Aynnie McMinns. It was bits and pieces of one woman's life and her legacy to me, the daughter-in-law she did not live long enough to meet.

I climbed those 14 steps to the attic almost every day but I told no one. I liked keeping it to myself and that is how my life turned out to be clandestine and grew like Topsy.

CHAPTER 1

Broughton, Georgia
June 20, 2015

Standing next to the antique Cheval mirror, I slipped on one of the scanty Victoria Secrets undergarments given to me along with appropriate smirks at a bridal shower. My friends had done everything they could think of to turn me into a hot vamp on my honeymoon night. As I gazed at myself in the mahogany oval frame, I thought I did indeed look rather vampish and I smiled knowing that Jake would approve.

The mirror easily enfolded my five-foot two-inch body on that special day, the one on which I was to become Mrs. Jake McMinns. Oh how all of my emotions catapulted that day. One minute I was sentimental, the next temperamental. Excited, too, more than I had ever been before in my life.

"OMG," gushed my best friend, Jillie. "When Jake gets a load of you in that thing, girl, he's gonna need CPR." She giggled. "You do remember how to administer CPR, don't you? Ha! Silly question. You, of all people, know exactly how to resuscitate that man." She giggled again.

I posed in front of the mirror, lingering for a moment. Pushing my breasts together and tightening the straps of the lace underwire bra, I sighed. "Why didn't I get a boob job? Tweedledee and Tweedledum trying to look sexy in an over-priced push-up bra ain't working."

Jillie shook her head and sighed. "Jake won't care about size as long as your girls are available when he wants them to be. What you shoulda done is learn how to cook."

I laughed. "I'll try to remember that, oh wise one blessed with superior knowledge of the opposite sex."

Jillie was always shy around everyone except me, never concerned if she didn't have a Saturday night date. If Jillie's prom nights were spent alone, it didn't seem to bother her. She would simply pop a batch of popcorn, turn on the TV and munch until the ball dropped in Times Square. I have always been envious of Jillie's self-reliance.

The two of us have been best friends forever but sisters only after my parent's untimely deaths. They were victims of the 9/11 disasters. Jillie and I were twelve-years-old at the time.

My mother and father had been flying to Los Angeles on that fateful

2001 day after visiting old friends who had recently moved from Georgia to Boston. Their plans were to tour Southern California for a few days followed by a drive up the coast to explore the wine country, a dream trip they had planned and looked forward to for years.

I found out about the Trade Center collapse as I was walking down the hall at school on the way to my next class. A friend of mine stopped to say, "Did you hear? We're being attacked by terrorists. They blew up a plane full of people in New York and everybody on it was killed."

My parents had boarded an early morning flight in Boston headed for Los Angeles, not New York. I was understandably shocked at the horrible news while at the same time relieved that it was not the plane my parents were on. Curious to find out the details of what had happened, I ducked into the principal's office and found the entire staff glued to CNN.

When a newscaster said, "American Airlines Flight 11 out of Boston," the room began to spin, my knees buckled and I fainted.

After the catastrophe, Jillie's mom and dad, long-time friends of my parents, petitioned the courts for guardianship and I became their "other" daughter. What a blessing it was. I had been an only child with no other family, not even an aunt or an uncle. Getting through that horrible period of my life, the awful grief and incessant nightmares, was made possible because I was loved and supported unconditionally by Jillie and her parents.

My non-related sister held up the wedding dress. Scattered with seed pearls and sequins, over twenty yards of silk made up the gown. "Lucky you that your mother was the same size you are. This dress is outrageous and you will look so beautiful in it. Totally da bomb."

I rolled my eyes. "Well it would look a whole lot better if I had big boobs."

There was a soft knock on the door followed by Jillie's mother's voice. "Are y'all decent in there?"

"Until around midnight tonight, and then all bets are off," I muttered and we both laughed.

"Come on in, Mom," Jillie and I called out together.

Margaret Scott's head peeked around the doorframe followed moments later by the rest of her trim body. One look at the future bride in her sexy undergarments and she exclaimed, "Oh my goodness, Cassie. Look at you, girl. You are in for some big trouble tonight."

"God's ears," I laughed. "Come help me get this bunch of silk over my head without messing up my hair, will you? I can't trust your daughter not to put my wedding dress on me backwards, upside down and inside out."

"Would not," Jillie quipped.

"Would, too." I grinned at my best friend.

Minutes later, the three of us stood in front of the antique mirror gazing at a bride: a bride that looked a whole lot like me.

Margaret held up the exquisite veil worn years before by my mother. "Cassie, your momma would be thrilled to pieces knowing that you're getting married in her wedding dress. You look so beautiful."

I turned to her. "Thank you, Mags. It means a lot to me for you to say that. More than you know. You always were and always will be my other mother, you know."

Tears swam in Margaret's eyes. "Oh! I hate like hell that you're moving up to North Carolina. How are we going to get along without you? Are you quite sure you want to leave us?"

I looked at the only woman ever coming close to replacing my real mother. "Tell you what, Mags, if you can talk Jake into moving to Georgia, I will back you up from here to heaven." I sighed. "Alas, I don't see that happening. My man is a North Carolinian through and through."

Two hours later, I walked slowly down the aisle to join my North Carolina State former linebacker-turned-lawyer. Our vows were said in front of admiring friends from both states, although notably absent and sorely missed by both of us were our two sets of parents.

Jake's mother, a widow for several years, had died three years before Jake and I met and like me, he was an only child. He inherited the family home in Bear River Falls, North Carolina after his mother's death.

It took over a year for the renovations to be finished, but the house to which Jake McMinns intended to live in with his bride looked less like the home of a little old lady and more the style of an up and coming small town attorney.

Jake was certain that providence placed me in his path of life. We met just days after the renovations on his house were done. I was the love of his life, he told me, and he also said that he and the house had been working in tandem just waiting for me.

I am a sucker for schmaltz.

Gazing at my groom while I cakewalked down the aisle on our wedding day, I had the urge to run into his waiting arms, decorum be damned. I didn't want to wait one minute longer to say, "I do," and go with him to Western North Carolina and my first real home.

I had no way of knowing that the journey I was about to take would crisscross distance and time in a way I never imagined.

CHAPTER 2

When I ask Jake what kind of things are stored upstairs in the attic, his reaction surprises me.

"I have no idea and furthermore I don't want to know. It's been years since I went up there and for good reason. The place creeps me out. You poke around all you want to, but don't expect me to go with you."

"Why, Jake McMinns! I'm shocked. Surely you can deal with a few old spooks." I grin.

"Cassie, my darling, haven't you figured out by now that I don't like anything over fifty-years-old? That's why I married you." He grins back at me.

Touché.

I protest and try not to whine. "There might be antiques or other things we could bring down and use. You said your mother appreciated nice things, so she probably stored what she wasn't using at the moment in the attic. People do that, you know. Store things in the attic? Don't you think she would want us to take a look just in case we could use something of hers?"

"You have got to be kidding, Cassie. Trust me, there's nothing worth a damn up there except maybe the value of a tax write-off after we donate it all to the Salvation Army." He sighs. "I don't really want anything up there because it's all junk. People do that, you know. Store junk in the attic?"

He cocks his eyes at me while lifting both eyebrows Groucho Marx style. It is a poor imitation but I laugh anyway.

In the next moment, while I'm glaring at him, he has another thought. His expression changes and I notice it right away.

"Hold on a minute. I just remembered that the other day I needed some information and couldn't find it anywhere. Since you've brought the attic to mind, I'm wondering if what I was looking for might be up there. It didn't occur to me before, but if Mama didn't toss it, she probably stored it in the attic."

A grin tries to escape from my lips, but I hold it back. After my husband leaves his law office for the day, it isn't often he shows a spark of interest in anything other than sex or ESPN. Mostly he wants not to think so I remind myself that miracles do happen.

"Hey, let's go up there and look for it, Jake. If we do it together, we'll ward off those pesky spooks," I say. "Are you going to tell me what you were looking for or not? It's your little black book, isn't it? Telephone numbers, boob measurements, how many times you scored—sexy photos of Scarlett Johansson? No? "

He pulls his recliner up to a sitting position and massages the back of his neck, a thing he does to rid himself of the tension he carries in his neck and shoulders.

I wait.

"Scarlett Johansson. Don't I wish." He shakes his head and grins. "Mama kept a football She probably got rid of it after I graduated. No reason for her to hang onto it."

"What a dumb-ass thing to say, Jake. Mothers don't throw things like that away, especially after going to the trouble of keeping it for four years. Come upstairs with me and let's look for it. I'd kinda like to see pictures of you dressed up like Kobe Bryant."

He pushes the recliner back down with a resounding thunk, closes his eyes and takes a deep breath. "Kobe plays basketball, not football. Besides, Cassie, I told you. I don't want anything to do with that attic. I deal with old clients and all of their old stuff every time I draw up a Will. When I walk through that door at night, the last thing I want to look at is more old stuff. Is that so hard for you to understand?"

"But what about the scrapbook?"

He massages his neck again, turning it side to the other in a slow roll. "What about it? I don't need to look at it again. Hell, I lived it."

"Jake, you're pissing me off. I told you I want to see that scrapbook and do you know why? Because, dear heart, before I went out with you, I never dated a jock because I thought they were all Neanderthals. Then you came along and showed me how wrong I was. I made a judgment call based on misguided information and it was silly of me to ever have thought it."

His eyes remain closed. "I am an EX-jock, and maybe you weren't so wrong after all."

"I want to see that scrapbook, dammit. It's a part of your life I know nothing about and I want to know everything there is to know about the man I married. Is that so hard for you to understand?"

He cut his eyes at me. "It was no big deal, Cassie. Seriously."

"Then why were you looking all over for the scrapbook?"

He is quiet for a moment. "I was trying to get information on one of my teammates. We were good friends in college but we lost track of each other after graduation. Cassie, I'm going to say this once and I want you to hear me: don't make this out to be important because it's not. If the scrapbook is in the attic and if you happen to run across it, then by all means, bring it down and I'll look through it. Maybe I can find the info I need. If it's not there, don't sweat it because I'm not going to."

He closes his eyes, tenses his jaw and folds his arms across his chest, body language that clearly screams his thoughts on the discussion. As I gaze at him in his "subject closed position," I wonder if there is something in the attic that goes deeper than he's willing to admit. I'll bet an old football scrapbook has nothing whatsoever to do with it so I can't help but think he is hiding something from me. Maybe not Scarlett Johansson's vital statistic, but something.

He clears his throat. "If you go plundering around up there and decide to clear it out, you're gonna need help getting things downstairs for the Salvation Army or Goodwill to pick up. I can hire somebody to do that for you. I don't want you lifting heavy things and hurting yourself. One of my clients is good at that kind of thing and he could use the work."

He turns up the volume on macho man's sports world, known to every woman on the planet as ESPN.

I retrieve the novel I need to read for book club, open it and then try to get my head into it, but my thoughts keep floating up to the attic instead. After a few minutes, I snap the book closed and leave Jake in the den engrossed in the Lakers game. My guess is he probably doesn't even know I left the room.

Upstairs, I fill our large bathtub with hot water and soften it by adding an extra measure of bath oil. A hot bath is the best thing in the world to help me relax me and think. I consider going back down and brewing a cup of chamomile tea to sip while in the tub, but decide a glass of Merlot would be a quicker picker upper. I slip back downstairs to get what was left in the bottle after dinner.

Easing my body into the steaming water, I feel myself beginning to respond to nature's organic tranquilizer. My thoughts return downstairs, however, when I realize I want to rehash the conversation I'd had with Jake. That whole thing about a creepy attic doesn't make a lick of sense and, try as I might, I can't understand his over-reaction. It was so unlike the man I thought I knew so well.

Bottom line: I can't shake the feeling that there is something in the attic Jake doesn't want to see or hear about, something he refuses to acknowledge. Apparently, it is also something he has no plans to discuss with me.

I have to ask myself why it is that I even want to go through his mother's lifetime of jettisoned stuff. We have been married less than a year and by some standards I am still a bride with a lot of nesting to do, recipes to collect, meals to cook.

Maybe the best thing to do is simply forget about the attic so things in the past can stay in the past where they belong. We have plenty of furnishings. Do we really need another piece of furniture or more china and crystal? Why should I climb 14 steps just to plunder through a bunch of discarded relics? The attic is not going anywhere so it'll be there whenever or if ever I decide to check it out.

Draining my glass of wine in one big gulp, I slip down into the warm bath water until my shoulders are covered over. I sigh and tell myself again that maybe I will poke around up there one of these days. Like in a year or so.

I'm not sure whether it is the what-the-hell Merlot or the warm bath-oiled water, but one or the other helps me close the attic door in my mind where it remains tightly shut for another two weeks.

CHAPTER 3

I spend half a day trying with no success to rearrange furniture in one of the guest bedrooms. No matter how I shuffle things around, nothing seems to work. I stand back and consider the size of the bed, end tables and chest of drawers. I move each piece around again in my head and even draw it on a piece of paper before it finally dawns on me that the room is the perfect size and location for a future nursery. What nurseries need is a good rocking chair and I'll bet there is one in the attic.

It has been raining since late yesterday afternoon—slushy, messy and cold—winter weather that makes me want to curl up with a meaty mystery novel while soft baroque music plays in the background.

I stand just inside the doorway and gaze at that bedroom slash future nursery, and it's easy as pie to hear the walls when they whisper my name: Cassie. Cassie. Cassie.

The dreary weather outside dims the little bit of natural lighting on the stairway so I have to fumble around for a switch. Once I am bathed in light, I begin to climb the first of the 14 step to the attic.

I reach the top and expect it to be a jumble of discarded things too useful to be thrown away and no longer good enough to be on display in the living area of the house. But when I look around, I am shocked.

The light I'd switched on at the bottom of the stairway also turned on all of the lights throughout the attic. What I am calling an attic is no ordinary burial ground for abandoned stuff. It is huge, divided into individual rooms with fourteen-foot high ceilings. It is in perfect order as if someone had lived there only yesterday.

In the main room, the largest of them all, a basketball goal has been erected, a section of the wood floor painted bright red as if to designate the playing area. To the side of the "basketball court," I see a pinball machine and easily imagine a long ago stream of colored lights blinking on and off in manic rotation.

Over to one side, a shuffleboard court is charted on the floor in red, white and green, complete with triangles and numbers. Never having been much into sports, I'm not sure what any of it is all about so I make a mental note to ask Jake. My need at the moment is simply to take it all in so I can ask Jake without sounding like a ninny.

A card table with four chairs surrounding it sits underneath a double window. Two decks of playing cards are in the middle of the table as if waiting for a dealer and boxes of board games are stacked neatly over to one side. Monopoly, Chinese Checkers, Chutes and Ladders, Candyland

and Clue are the ones that catch my eye, but there are dozen more,

Doing a 360, I realize that there's another room off from the main one. The downstairs light switch had lit it up also with two softly glowing lamps on both sides of an old brass bed. The bed is made up with pillows packed into. A dust ruffle sweeps the floor. On top of the mattress, a quilt stitched in the wedding ring pattern is spread. In one corner, there's a wing chair covered in soft chintz; a matching ottoman is placed in front of it. A floor lamp behind the chair gives off a soft bit of light as though inviting me to sit down and stay for a while.

The floors in the big, outer room are of bare wood, but the bedroom floor is covered in wall-to-wall blue, plush carpet. I have an urge to kick off my shoes and sink my feet into it.

Soft yellow and blue striped wallpaper enhance the coziness of this room.

One window looks out to the street three floors below. It is curtained with ruffled white organdy and tied back so that the light of day can filter through. An antique barrister's bookcase, the stackable kind like in Jake's law office has been placed underneath the window.

Not wanting to leave the warmth of this snug little room, I force myself to continue my exploration. There is still so much more to discover and I am beyond curious to find out what might be behind the closed door next to the cozy little bedroom.

When I open that door the room is dark. Apparently it was not wired on the same light connections as the other rooms. An automatic switch has been installed, however. It is the kind found on refrigerator doors. As soon as I open the heavy six-paneled outer door, the entire room is suddenly lit with so much track lighting that it makes me squint.

What surprises me the most is that there is only one item in the room strategically placed so that it sits right in the middle as if to insure that it won't be overlooked. Four bright track lights shine directly down on that one item which turns out to be an old humpback trunk.

I open the lid and pick up a box filled with brittle snapshots falling from the black pages of an old scrapbook. A quick look tells me that there are no football photos of Jake in it so I avoid further handling of the torn, yellow newspaper clippings for fear of destroying what is left of them. I do the same for other old paper keepsakes that might crumble at my touch.

A pair of bronzed baby shoes I assume had been Jake's is underneath the box. The inscription, although dark and difficult to make out, tells me the shoes belonged to someone, but not Jake. I find a framed Episcopal confirmation certificate dated 1915, as well as a first grade primer illustrated with pictures of Dick, Jane, Sally and Puff on the cover, a

1947 edition.

In addition to the old newspaper clippings and sepia photos, there are some items placed underneath the box. They are intact, neatly placed and seemingly organized, as if placed there with a definite purpose in mind. When I reach down and lift out one of them, I find there is an envelope attached to it. What this?

Before I can answer my own question something else snatches my attention. I'm surprised I did not see it first thing.

Placed at the very top on the inside of the trunk is a stack of boxes. Each one is white with a white envelope attached to it, some large enough to hold an 8 x 10 inch photo with room to spare, others not so big. I have a feeling the first one might contain a guide to the contents in the trunk. I hope so.

Opening the envelope I expect to find such an index, but instead I see a letter addressed to, 'To the woman married to my son.'

I figure the woman in question, at least on this particular day, has to be me.

CHAPTER 4

Hello to Jake's Wife!

I am taking a wild guess that if you are opening this letter than you are the woman who has married him (and I do hope you are). Let me start off by introducing myself. I am Jake's mother, Aynnie McMinns. How do you do?

About now you are probably saying to yourself, "I thought she was dead." Well, as I write this, I am still very much alive, but if you are reading it, then I am not. If you think I'm a nut case for writing a letter like this, that's okay. You are not the first. I have always tried to represent the lighter side of this family so it is important to me, especially now, to enjoy the time I have left.

On the other hand, like many others, I am forced by fate to deal with my share of heartache and disappointment. For instance, I had hoped to live long enough to see my son happily married, but obviously that didn't happen. Lord knows, I waited as long as God would allow. But, as often is the case, His agenda trumped mine.

When you saw this old trunk I bet you never expected to find letters written to you inside of it. The reason I chose to address you in particular is because I figured Jake would sooner let the house burn to the ground before he would go through things left in the attic. As much as I love my son, he doesn't have one iota of interest in family history. Never has. I knew he wouldn't look through this trunk, but I figured if and when he got married, perhaps it would fall to his wife to do it.

Jake was carrying on one evening not long ago about something that happened that day in court. He was being very lawyerly, much like his father used to be, and his behavior gave me the idea to put together a history of the McMinns family—the good, bad and even the ugly. Jake would never do it himself because there are too many things in his past he refuses to think about, let alone acknowledge. How do I know this? Because I am his mother.

That means, like they say in the movies, it's just you and me, kid. If you stick with this little project of mine, you will learn all you ever need to know about this family. I promise to give you an honest account and I hope it won't bore you into the middle of next week.

Lord, how I wish I had lived long enough to see that boy married. I had just about given up on him until the night I had an incredible dream.

In it, Jake had found the love of his life and it was a perfect match—the two of them fit together like a pair of bookends. In my dream, I watched them go hand-in-hand down a winding path, laughing, talking and teasing each other. I woke up happy, knowing somehow that I had been given a glimpse of my son's future. It took Jake a long time to find you, darlin', so you must be someone very special.

I had that dream a few months before I got sick. Since I was diagnosed, I have devoted many days to gathering meaningful things I felt would give you a sense of family. The truth is, I never thought I'd be taking a fast train out of here because I'm not old enough to die. I had thought I would celebrate my hundredth birthday but then the Big Conductor in the Sky punched my ticket on that fast train out of here.

Everything you'll find in the trunk had great value to me at one time, but if you are expecting a treasure chest full of money, you'll be disappointed. The truth is, you might think it's all trivial nonsense and wonder why I bothered to save any of it. I hope that doesn't happen because there are lives inside this trunk and years of memories. Not just mine, but others who came before me. I think of the O'Connor/McMinns history as a mixed bag of souls spanning the generations—an unfinished patchwork quilt waiting just for you, Jake's bride.

I attached notes or letters of explanation to most of the items, but I may have forgotten one or two. The important ones are there, I'm sure of that. They will explain each thing so that you can to pass it on down, if you should choose to do so. Who knows? Maybe you'll get to know the mother-in-law you never met. You might even learn to love me a little and if you do, I hope that you will introduce my son to a side of me I am convinced he never knew.

Please look at all the memorabilia collected inside the trunk as well as other things scattered all over the attic. Study it all before you decide to throw it away. Hold it, smell its history, read what I wanted you to know.

At this point I suspect you are overwhelmed and probably need some time, maybe even another day or two to process it all. Take all the time you need. We, that is, the trunk, the attic and I, will be right here when you decide to return to us.

With love from Aynnie

Cassie

Aynnie is right. I have to stop and catch my breath. Jake's suggestion that we donate to a charity might turn out to be the best way to deal with all of this. So we either call the Salvation Army or figure out a way to lug everything downstairs and hold an overdue estate sale.

Yet when I gaze around the cavernous outer room and think about what I just read in Aynnie's letter, a palpable calmness seems to settle throughout the attic as well as within me.

Instead of seeing the room as a unit, I look at each item individually because I want to take it all in. Finding the mysterious trunk in the smaller, track-lit room distracted me for a while. By taking a second look I realize how much my perception shifted from when I walked up those stairs less than an hour ago. It's not just my perception of the attic that's changed, it is also how I now view Jake's mother. I will never think of her in the same way again.

Jake doesn't often speak of her, but on one occasion he related some quirky little thing she had done and in the telling, he seemed to be almost apologetic. Since I had never known the woman, I accepted his assessment of her without questioning him further, although I didn't understand it. It seemed to me that he had passed sentence on her for the terrible crime of being herself and his judgment was not kind.

Jake said his mother was a maverick that thumbed her nose at convention. So what? It sounded to me like she had been fun, and at the time he told me the offhand story, I wished I had known her.

Not really wanting to wait another day to keep going as Aynnie suggested, I pick up the letter she wrote and begin to read the PS on the second page.

CHAPTER 5

P.S.

Dear Jake's Bride,

I am glad you came back. I have so much I want to tell you.

When you married my son, you became not just a member of a good family but a solid part of it. Both the O'Connor's and the McMinns' have always garnered respect from the community, the rich as well as the poor. I believe the legacy left behind by our families is one of integrity. You can be very proud that you have become the newest McMinns woman.

I have placed a thin, rather small box under the envelope containing this letter. I did it on purpose because the item inside is where you need to begin as you embark on the journey to discover the McMinns family saga.

Go ahead now and open that box.

Aynnie

Cassie

It takes only a moment for me to find the long box Aynnie described. Pristine white, I realize that she had set it apart from the crackled collection of faded papers and photographs, more than likely to make sure I would not miss it.

Inside the box there is a handkerchief pinned in place in such a way that it cannot get creased or wrinkled. The handkerchief is white, edged in tatted lace and now yellowed around the edges. It is dainty, the linen noticeably thin in places. A lady would have stuffed it inside a dress sleeve or in a shallow pocket.

When I take the pins out and lift the handkerchief from the box, a lingering fragrance of lavender floats through the air. I smile. Jake's mother had loved lavender so much that she even bought all of her clothes in some variation of the color.

People in Bear River Falls called her the African violet wizard, or so I have been told. They would bring her violets gasping their last breath, and she would nurse them back to health. Some of her prize violets are struggling to survive at my kitchen window, and even today our bathroom holds a faint but distinctive bouquet of the lavender soaps she used.

Jake scoffed at his mother's love of lavender telling me it was only one of her obsessions. "Momma's Purple Passion was just one of her many idiosyncrasies."

I examine the handkerchief again and when I do, my need to know and my curiosity grows in direct proportion to everything I've learned. I can't imagine why a piece of cloth was so important that Aynnie wanted it to be first in line, but something tells me I am about to find out.

CHAPTER 6

"There is a sacredness in tears.
They are not the mark of weakness, but of power.
They speak more eloquently than ten thousand tongues.
They are messengers of overwhelming grief
and unspeakable love." ~Washington Irving

Dear Jake's Bride,

What you have in your hand is the traditional family bridal handkerchief given to me by my mother the day I became Mrs. James Donovan McMinns. The handkerchief has been passed down to all of the brides in Momma's family for I don't know how many generations. Since I was the only O'Connor daughter and I never had daughters of my own, I planned to give the handkerchief to Jake's bride. To you. I think it was Woody Allen who said, 'If you want to make God laugh, tell him about your plans.' Well ...

I had so hoped to see you carry the handkerchief on your wedding day as the "something old." But that wasn't the main thing, just as it wasn't when my mother gave it to me. I wanted you to have the handkerchief to dab away the tears of happiness that I knew you would shed on your wedding day.

I was so young when James and I got married and so much in love. I was a nice Irish girl who didn't know anything about real life. Nothing! An insufferable romantic, I thought as soon as I got married life would automatically become idyllic. A happy, happy, happy ever after.

I couldn't cook with a toot, but still I imagined myself serving meals while dressed in high-heel shoes and crisp organdy aprons to protect my good clothes. James, I was certain, would look away from my perfect fantasy gourmet dinners and openly admire his stylish wife. Yep. That fantasy walked right down the aisle with me. Was my head stuck up my you-know-where or what?

This is how naive I was: I believed that when I got pregnant maybe I would experience a bit of morning sickness for a few days but then it would pass. I would soon blossom like a rose and all because of the new life growing inside of me. Giving birth, I thought, might be a little bit uncomfortable ... like maybe going to the dentist.

If that wasn't silly enough, I also believed that emotionally James and I would remain in our original state of bliss and nothing could or would alter it. Nobody told me that being "in love" only lasts until reality sets in. I found out the hard way that marriage requires work and lots of it. I wish someone had given me a heads up about living with another person because for all the years we were married, it was a challenge to every brain cell in my silly head.

How totally unprepared I was to be a wife, how tragic I felt. But then one day I remembered my mother did give me the heads up I needed when she gave me the traditional wedding handkerchief. That realization came one dreary, cold January afternoon as I rocked young Jake, then recovering from a bad case of pneumonia. While he slept in my arms, I used the time to think about my life and, if not all of them, then at least some of my illusions.

For over a week Jake was sick as a dog and I had stayed up with him night after night, sleeping next to him whenever either of us was able to sleep. No need to say that I was out of my mind with concern for my child. Three times we almost lost him, but thanks to a merciful God the child's fever finally broke. By that time, of course, I was a wreck.

As I rocked and sang his favorite songs, the worn out child finally gave in to exhaustion and fell asleep in my arms. I kept holding him, rocking, not wanting to put even the tiniest distance between his little body and my own. I must have been rocking him for hours when the tears I had held back began to fall. I rocked and cried, rocked and cried. In fact, I cried about everything that day.

With my baby boy heavy in my arms and tears going haywire down my face, I fumbled for the wedding handkerchief Mother had given me, the one that is now in your possession. I had made it a habit to stuff it in my pocket each morning as surely as I slipped into clean underwear.

While I wiped away salty tears, Momma's words came rushing back as clearly as if she were standing next to me with her hand on Jake's sweet brow. I felt as if I could almost see her loving, understanding smile and that was the moment when I remembered the words she said to me on my wedding day.

Cassie

I stop reading and put down her letter, hoping, needing to rest my mind for a moment. My spine is tingly and it sounds crazy. I can feel Aynnie's spirit hovering next to me, much like how she felt her own mother's presence while rocking the sleeping Baby Jake that day.

In many ways I am awed knowing that she planned this out with the sole intention of helping me to become a full-fledged member of the McMinns family. What she could not have known is how wonderful it has made me feel to know that she graced me with such a loving feeling of acceptance.

I wonder, had my own mother been aware of her impending death would she have been as generous with our family history?

I take a deep breath and allow it escape slowly like I learned to do in yoga class. Since this has all been very strange and unexpected, I probably should heed Aynnie's earlier suggestion and back off for a day or so.

But how can I leave before learning about the handkerchief that was supposed to have been mine the day I became Cassie McMinns? I want to know its secrets and not only that, I have to find out about the power hidden within the folds of the wedding handkerchief. I'm hooked.

But before I can read any more of the letter, I glance at my watch.

"Good lord," I cry out loud. It is past time for Jake to be home and I haven't started to cook dinner or anything. There is no way I am comfortable telling him what I discovered in the same attic he wants nothing to do with.

The handkerchief and all of the secrets it holds will have to wait until tomorrow.

After kissing Jake goodbye, I stand at the back door and wave like a good wife straight out of the Nineteen Fifties. He will be in Asheville almost all day taking depositions, so I will be free to wander through decades of the McMinns history. Yea!

His car has not yet turned the corner when I take the stairs two at a time up to the attic. I pick up the part of the letter I did not read yet and begin where I left off yesterday.

***

Aynnie

My mother felt it was her place to counsel me, and I suppose that was what mothers did for their daughters back in the day. She said I would feel heartbroken at times and then she said to me, 'You will be so certain that you are unloved, unappreciated and taken for granted. You'll think of your past loves and wonder: What If? But those moments will be few and temporary. They will pass, and if you have a lick of sense, you'll learn from them and let them go.'

Her words to me were meaningless at the time, but I did learn the lessons eventually. Call it trial by fire, but is there a better teacher than life itself? In any case, and with the full realization that I don't come close to knowing all the answers, I believe it is now my turn to pass along my mother's wisdom. Maybe my words will make some of your days easier than some of mine were for me. If you will allow it, I promise you that this little handkerchief will always be there for you when your emotions are going haywire. Trust me on this; I speak from experience.

My dear, you will shed tears of elation the day you feel new life inside of you, thrilled that a separate soul was forged from the love you and Jake have for each other. You will be devoted to this child of yours with every scintilla of love ever felt by every mother who ever lived.

Grateful tears will fall as your child gasps his first breath, and when you count his tiny fingers and toes and thank Almighty God for this small bundle of perfection. You will weep as the two of you discover each other during your first moments alone, when you hold your baby's face close to yours allowing him to taste your own tears.

There will be tears of pride the day he says 'Momma' for the first time; compassionate tears when he falls off the sliding board and comes running to you for solace and a Band-Aid.

It's not possible for me to remember how many times I spit on this handkerchief and then washed dirt smudges from Jake's little face while he squirmed. I am certain Jake felt many emotions while I was cleaning him up, but love for his mother was not one of them.

Your child's first day at school, heartbreak at not making the team or being shunned by his friends for no reason—those feelings will haunt you. They will render you sleepless and make you weep long into the night.

But as swiftly as your child's dwindling youth will fly, nothing can prepare you for the day he leaves home for good. You will ache in the very marrow of your bones as the sudden silence surrounds your house and shouts at you from every seam, crack and crevice.

Oh, look at me painting such a dark picture when that is not my intention at all. There will be many wonderful days for you to enjoy, each one memorable in its own way.

I'm merely hoping to prepare you for the less idyllic times when you are filled with deep-down loneliness, when the skies are covered over with dismal rain, when your husband works late into the night, when you need him and he is not there.

Days like that can drain your desire to do anything but sit down and cry your eyes out. If and when that happens, don't forget that this handkerchief will be there for you. It may be small, but it is large enough to hold all of your tears.

You will need it the morning you glance in the bathroom mirror and discover your first gray hair, and later when you find yourself longing for the seasons of your youth.

This wedding handkerchief will be waiting for you when your aging body no longer responds to your commands or when you are sick and your children forget to call. It will also catch your grateful tears when your husband becomes aware that the kids hurt your feelings when they didn't call so he brings you Campbell soup and burnt toast on a tray.

Some days something will tickle you and make you laugh so hard that tears roll down your cheeks with complete abandon. It happens to me when I watch I Love Lucy re-runs. It cracks me up every time Lucy and Ethel stomp those grapes.

There may be times in your marriage when you fear that Jake loves another instead of you, when the two of you can no longer talk without quarreling, when you are angry and need to lash out at him for stealing the girl who once lived inside of you.

But remember one thing: men have a tough time understanding a woman's need to cry. They don't get that it's our way of ridding ourselves of emotional toxins, stumbling blocks to healthy living. Forgive them. They just can't help it.

By passing the wedding handkerchief and its traditions on to you, I hope you will think of it as a source of strength, strange as that may sound. You see, this simple piece of cloth has embodied many lives over many years. It has been washed hundreds of times in a woman's tears, mine, my mother's, even her mother's before her. If you keep it close to you, you will learn to cherish all the lives it holds within. More often than you can possibly know at this moment, the past is the one thing that can always shine a new light and show you the way when you feel lost.

Although I have given you a great deal to think about, hopefully it hasn't been too much. You are now in possession of the O'Connor wedding handkerchief, the last piece of memorabilia I am placing in the trunk in order for you to find it first. I feel secure in the knowledge that this small legacy will be stored safely in the pocket of your clothes as well as your heart until it becomes your turn to pass it on.

It has taken me quite a while to assemble all the things you will find in the trunk and even more time to chronicle the background for each of the items. My time on earth is winding down more quickly than I would like for it to, but I feel I am leaving something valuable for you, the newest McMinns woman. With that thought in mind, I will leave you now knowing that I can and will rest in peace.

With love from Aynnie.

Cassie

I sit cross-legged on the bare attic floor under the illogical bank of track lights and I weep.

***

Two weeks pass before I climb the stairs to the attic again although I often walked by the door, paused, and then fought the impulse to drop everything I needed to do in order to go back up there.

Because of Aynnie and her legacy to me, I now consider the McMinns History Trunk to be an exclusive place meant only for me so I have been itching to leave my real life behind in order to embrace the one that exists only between the two of us.

What kept me from doing what I longed to do was my other life. It kept getting in the way.

The Christmas party at Jake's law firm is a tradition each year, held in part to welcome the new associates in addition to celebrating the holiday season. The partner's take turns hosting the event and this year it happens to be Jake's turn at bat. In other years, it was often held at the Country Club but this year Jake insisted on hosting it at our home.

"How about it, Cass? You can handle a cocktail party, right?"

Our chats by the fire while he drinks his end of the day Jack Daniels and I sip my glass of wine or an occasional martini, have taken on a comfortable regularity. It has become our time to reconnect with each other while we laugh at and share our individual day. The cocktail party idea is something that Jake threw at me from left field.

"Yikes, Jake! When did you decide this? And how long do I have to get ready for it?"

As it turned out, I had ample time to call the caterer, hire a bartender and get the house cleaned up. Piece of fruitcake. And the party was a wonderful success and we both enjoyed it.

Getting everything ready meant decorating more than normal for Christmas. That, in addition to all the other things involved in hosting a party really cut into my time upstairs. I was so glad when the smoke finally cleared and I was once again free to wander through the years with my new mother-in-law, Aynnie.

The interesting thing was that each time I was about to go up to the attic and delve into the past with her, a pragmatic side of me slammed on the brakes. I would then tell myself to keep busy doing what I needed to do and wait for a rainy day or a blue mood, either of which was bound to come around sooner or later.

And that's just what happened today. It is Thursday afternoon and two weeks since Christmas came and went. Even the weatherman is being cooperative. The prediction for a typical January day, dreary with a light mist of rain, is expected to continue way into tomorrow.

I feed the cat and then go to the music system Jake installed in the house when he refurbished it. I select several Chopin CD's that I hope will waft through the downstairs rooms and into the attic. It's appropriate, I think, for an old friend and his music to accompany Aynnie and me on our continuing adventures. I leave the door open so that my selections of tranquil, romantic music can drift unfettered up the 14 steps to the attic.

I remember that the attic floor was cold when I sat down on it, so for this visit I bring along a cushion for padding my behind as well as keeping it warm. It is way more comfortable and I sigh contentedly the minute I sit down in front of the trunk in the small track-lit room.

Closing my eyes, I silently ask Aynnie to guide my hands in choosing the thing she wants me to find. My eyes are shut tight when something plops into my lap and just about scares me into the middle of next week. Miss Priss, our more than curious cat has discovered the open attic door. Whether it is curiosity or the need for company, I can't say, but it looks like she isn't going anywhere anytime soon.

"Dammit, Miss Priss," I yell. "Don't you ever do that again."

She looks at me as if to apologize but then quickly changes her mind, curls her body around in my lap until she is comfortable and ready for a snooze. What better place for a nosy feline, I think, than an attic rife with a semi-active spirit?

With Miss Priss purring softly in my lap and Arthur Rubinstein's heart pouring into a Chopin nocturne I sigh, close my eyes and lift the trunk lid.

Reaching inside, my hand touches yet another box and I know. It is only for a second but somehow, don't ask me how, I feel certain I have found the thing I am destined to find.

I open my eyes again and carefully take the box out of the trunk.

It is not as small as the previous box and it weighs a lot more. I put it down on the floor so that I can slit the tape with the end of my fingernail.

Aynnie had used lavender and pink tissue paper to wrap the small pieces I find inside of the box. The tissue paper feels as crisp as if she had placed it in the package only yesterday.

On the top of the tissue paper I find a large manila envelope and suspect that it will tell me everything I need to know about the contents of the second box.

CHAPTER 7

Dear Jake's Bride,

When I made the decision to organize this family jumble, I was unsure where to begin. I didn't want it to be a laundry list of boring genealogy, even though it would have been much easier than returning to a past I guarded for too a long time. The truth of the matter is, I can only write about my own experiences, things I lived through and learned from.

With that thought in mind, I realized that there was only one logical place to begin and that, of course, was at the beginning.

Packed inside this box, you will find a child's tea set that belonged to me when I was a little girl. You will recognize I am sure the familiar Blue Willow pattern since it's been around for ages. Many people associate it with a Blue Plate Special found in almost every café and diner across the country. As for me, I never ate a Blue Plate Special in my life, but now I wish I had. Maybe I will before I need to process all of my food in a blender.

On the other hand, I did have lots of tea parties using these pieces when I was a child. They were parties attended by Raggedy Ann, her brother Andy, and my twin sister, whom you will learn more about soon enough. We would sit around our small child's table on matching chairs, never realizing how lucky we were to have things like a table and four chairs meant only for playtime. Almost everything was scarce or rationed, you see, because of the war.

I asked Momma once if she would buy us some real tea and cookies so that we could have an authentic tea party. She looked at me like I had lost my mind. "I don't have enough rations for that kind of thing, Aynnie. There's a war going on."

So my sister and I learned to make believe. There will be much more about her in letters to come.

Eventually Dixie, who would in time become my best friend, joined the group and remained for several years. She filled a gaping hole that characterized my young life at a time when I desperately needed a friend. When Dixie told me that she handpicked me to be her best friend, I felt special. On occasion, she would substitute the words "bon amie," for friend, flaunting the little dab of French she said she claimed to have learned. It hardly mattered since no one but me could hear her speak in any language. I was also the only one who could see her.

Dixie often reminded me that she was of Virginia heritage and that she had been raised accordingly. "My people can be traced all the way back to Thomas Jefferson," she would say. It was Dixie who told me once that it was a crying shame that I knew next to nothing about proper tea parties, but that it was time I learned a thing or two. After that, the playhouse tea parties took on a more formal air.

This is so silly to me now as I write about it. Fact of the matter is that it's been years since I even thought about those tea parties. Dixie's imaginary presence during that period of time, however, was probably responsible for my being able to handle the sadness that permeated our family for such a long time.

You may be wondering at this point why a little girl growing up in a safe, affluent environment, would ever need to learn how to handle sadness. Good question.

You see, I had a twin sister, Laynnie, but hardly any other children to play with. We had each other, though, and like two peas in a pod, it was enough for us. We were happy as long as we were able to have our frequent tea parties in the playhouse or while doing almost anything together.

Our mother was not the most patient person with children, so I am sure she loved the fact that we were entertaining ourselves in the playhouse and not underfoot. As long as we were busy doing things together and we didn't whine or complain, she was happy. As a result, even though we often wished for the companionship of other kids, we managed to remain the way Momma liked it: nice, quiet, polite little girls who knew better than to bug their mother.

One afternoon after lunch, my sister and I were outside playing on the hill in front of our house. It was a fine, crisp afternoon in mid-October, and we managed to run up and down the hill so many times that we both were out of breath. I had a side ache but Laynnie, who had the energy of ten children, kept on running up and down the hill even as I lagged behind.

That particular day, she reached the top of the hill before I did (as expected). She turned around with a wide grin plastered on her face—I can still see her. She cupped her hands around her mouth and shouted, "I won! I won! I'm the Queen of the Hill!"

I waved to her, a signal to acknowledge her triumph and continued reign as Queen, and then I stooped down to tie my shoe. When I looked up again, Laynnie was already out of sight. In no particular hurry, I stopped to pick a few dandelions before trudging the rest of the way up the hill. I made wishes and blew all of the feathery petals off every one of the weeds I picked.

When I reached the top of the hill, it was just in time to watch a woman shove my sister into an old car that I didn't recognize. Laynnie was kicking hard at the woman and screaming my name. "Aynnie! Aynnie! Help me!"

I didn't understand what was happening—I was just a child, after all. I didn't know what to do or how to go about doing it. The experience was surreal, a bad dream, a terrible nightmare. I stood still hoping to wake up, I suppose, or maybe I was thinking that an adult would come along and take care of things.

It wasn't until the car with my sister inside of it sped down the street, around the corner and out of sight, that I burst out of my stupor.

In less than thirty minutes, police surrounded the entire neighborhood and our house spilled over with people. The authorities came first, of course, followed by some of Daddy's lawyer friends and other people from his office.

As soon as I came to my senses, I had run home screaming. I was crying so hard that I couldn't even tell Momma what had happened until she calmed me down. Right away, she picked up the phone and called Daddy to let him know what happened.

When she hung up the phone, she stood quite still for a moment and then she screamed. Just after that, her body buckled and she fell to the floor sobbing. I tried to get her to stop crying but I couldn't, so I became hysterical all over again. She looked at me with those huge tears streaming down her face, and she must have realized how much I needed her right then, so she pulled me into her lap right there on the floor and rocked me back and forth while we both cried.

That is how Daddy found us when he got home.

The rest of that day was awful. It was as if a dark cloud had come into our home to live and we had no choice but to allow it to remain. I remember that a doctor came and gave Momma a shot and told her it was for her own good. She looked at him and nodded but it was as though she was looking all the way through him.

Soon after the shot, Momma got real woozy. Pearl, our housekeeper, pulled Daddy to the side. "You go on and do what you got to do, Mr. O'Connor. I'll take care of Miz Mary and Aynnie, too. You got enough to worry 'bout."

She took off my mother's shoes and covered her with lightweight afghan because by that time Momma was out cold. Pearl looked at me with those warm, compassionate eyes I had known all of my life. "Come here, little one. Pearl needs to hold you."

Well, she didn't have to ask me twice. Even today I remember the feeling I had of being wrapped in that woman's ample arms. I can still hear her saying, "Shhhh, now. Shhhh. It's gonna be all right, Aynnie. It's gonna be all right."

That night, I stayed awake for as long as my little body would allow, hoping beyond hope and praying like a Catholic that my sister Laynnie, my other self, would stroll through the door acting like nothing at all had happened. I had a vision of her laughing real loud and telling us that she had played the best practical joke of all on us.

I could hear her saying, "I'm the Queen of Practical Jokes," and I saw myself having to beg Daddy not to be mad or punish her for giving us all such a scare. I heard myself reminding him that she had come back home safe and sound and we should all be grateful.

But none of that happened.

The recounting of Laynnie's kidnapping is taking a larger bite out of my heart than I thought it would. I promise to tell you more about that awful time, as well as the significance of the Willow tea sets. But for now, I have to stop.

When I write again on this subject, it will be here in this same box along with the tea set.

With love from Aynnie

Cassie

I am so glad I don't have to read any more right now. Even though my curiosity is at an all-time high, I am pretty sure I would be unable to take in anything else. Just given the fact that Aynnie had a twin sister I've never heard of is enough to stop me cold. That the sister was kidnapped and Jake never even mentioned it seriously blows my mind. My brain is begging to be chilled.

I find it incredible that Jake didn't tell me about this. I have to wonder if it is possible that Jake knows nothing about it? Didn't his mother ever tell him about something so significant? There must be more to the kidnapping than meets the eye.

I slowly get up from my Gandhi position, stretch and moan aloud at the pleasure of unleashing cramped muscles. I have not worked out but once since beginning my attic adventures and my body is holding a rebellion, as well it should. Take me for a run, it shouts.

What a great idea. A good run will do wonders for my body, not to mention my totally confused brain. It will help me sort through some of the growing disquiet with regard to Jake's hidden family history.

But just as I am putting on my running shoes, the phone rings. As soon as I answer it, all thoughts of solitary exercise are immediately quashed.

"We're waiting for you, Cassie. Where are you? Aren't you coming?"

It is Anne Gerard, wife of Jake's law partner. Since Jake brought me to Bear River Falls, she has included me in everything from book club to delivering Meals on Wheels.

My stomach drops down, down, down to my toes.

"Coming?" The word comes out in a stammer. "Um ... coming where, Anne?"

An unpleasant pregnant pause gives way after a moment to Anne clearing her throat. "Cassie, you were supposed to bring refreshments to the book club today and we are all here waiting on you before we get started. Are you running late or what?"

Oh my lord. I had totally forgotten. Not only that, I had not even picked up the book I was supposed to have read, One Day in the Life of Ivan Denisovich. Hard for me to fathom, but some of the members are actually looking forward to discussing it. Refreshments? Hell's bells! Feeling as though I was hit over the head with a two by four, I finally remember that I promised to bring cookies. My name, what's left of it, just changed. In one single afternoon it went from Cassie to Dumb Shit.

"Anne, thanks for calling. I am running a little bit late because of ... of just that. I went out for a run and lost track of time."

It is a lie, but it's the best I can come up with on such short notice. "I just now got home. Tell the ladies to go ahead and start without me and I'll be there as soon as I change out of my sweaty running clothes. We can munch on cookies and drink lots and lots of coffee either during or after the book discussion, okay? I figure we'll need sugar and coffee because taking Solzhenitsyn apart is not for the faint hearted."

I hang up the phone. There it is again. My other life has an annoying habit of messing with me and screwing up my plans. I'm getting real sick of it.

The next morning as soon as Jake leaves for the office, I put a load of dirty clothes in the washer and fill Miss Priss's bowl with enough dry food to keep her chubby for a week. After that, I feel perfectly justified in making my way up those now familiar 14 steps to the attic because there is no way I will wait another day to find out about Aynnie's twin sister.

CHAPTER 8

Dear Jake's Bride,

I wish I knew your given name as opposed to the one I've attached to you which is much too generic. I picture you as a Martha, Virginia, Amy or Katherine but alas, I seem to be stuck calling you Jake's Bride as though it is your real name. I hope you understand. I have given some thought to addressing you as My Dear, for that is what you are, but even that doesn't seem to fit.

As promised, and with a huge apology for leaving things unfinished in my last note, I will tell you the rest of the story, as Paul Harvey says on his radio show. I hadn't realized the tenacity of my long-held emotional pain. It's amazing, however, the strength one can find while sipping a glass of wine. And so, I continue ...

***

When I woke up the morning after Laynnie was taken, I was aware that someone had tucked me into bed, probably Pearl. I noticed that I was wearing a white cotton gown with tatting on the collar and sleeves, one exactly like Laynnie's. I looked over at the twin bed next to mine and saw that it had not been slept in. Freddy Teddy, Laynnie's white bear, had not been moved from the pillow it rested on since Laynnie placed it there the morning before. After seeing that, my only thought was that my sister was gone and my heart was breaking.

The ransom note arrived in the mail that same day.

Momma and Daddy would have moved heaven and earth to get Laynnie back. How many times did I hear Daddy say that he would give up his own life or pay any amount of money for her safe return? In fact, he did pay quite a lot of money. The kidnappers demanded ten thousand dollars for my sister's safe return, a fortune back then.

Daddy didn't hesitate. He went straight to the bank for the cash, put it in a suitcase and left it at the drop site like the kidnappers had instructed him to do. He had to go alone late at night because he was warned not to involve the police. My parents didn't tell me the details at that time because of my youth; it was only later that I found out the kidnappers had threatened to take me also if the police were spotted anywhere near the drop site.

Daddy did exactly as he was told. He left a suitcase full of money in a cornfield fifteen miles outside of town and then he rushed home to sit by the telephone for the promised details on the return of my sister. None of it did any good because Laynnie never came home again. She was gone from us forever.

My parents were beyond distraught. For months, Momma walked around the house dazed and befuddled. She was unable to make decisions, even simple ones like whether to have Pearl cook peas or beans for supper. Before Laynnie was taken, Momma was known and admired as a beautiful woman, elegant in every way. During that period of boundless grief she didn't bother to comb her hair or wear powder, rouge or lipstick. I would be surprised if she even brushed her teeth most days. It was as though she had lost all sense of self when she lost her child.

"Momma," I asked her a few weeks after the ransom was paid, "why do you wear those bedroom slippers all the time? They're old and dirty."

She cocked her head to the side and looked at me with the vacuous stare to which I was becoming accustomed, then she turned around and walked out of the room. I don't know if I really expected an answer to my question, I just knew I wanted her to go back to being the person she used to be. A month or so went by before I noticed one day that she was no longer wearing those slippers. She had finally discarded them.

I'm guessing that Momma held a lot of guilt for Laynnie's disappearance since, as I wrote earlier, she wasn't the most patient or nurturing mother who ever lived. Hands-on parenting, I believe that's what it's called today, was never her strong suit. Apparently, it was far easier for her to become a blank page rather than deal with what happened to one of her daughters.

Daddy was not much better at it than she was. The grief inside of him never gave him a minute's reprieve. Unable to stop thinking about the kidnapping and what may or may not have been Laynnie's ultimate fate, the heartache he carried nearly did him in.

He sat in the straight-back chair next to the telephone from early morning until late at night. Pearl came in to cook for us every day, even though neither of my parents ate very much. In fact, Daddy had to be coaxed to leave the chair by the phone in order to sit with us at the table. It had always been his job to preside over our meals, to carve the meat with great ceremony before passing the plates so Momma could fill them with vegetables.

Following Laynnie's abduction, Daddy barely lifted his head once he was seated at the table. I was the one who said grace, not him and not Momma. He lost a lot of weight during that time, and so did Momma. She was skin and bones, a whisper of the woman she once was.

It looked like Daddy had no intention of returning to his law office and in fact, hardly even ventured outside of the house. During this awful time, he watched me like a birddog eyeing a prey. He needed to know where I was at any given moment of the day, demanding that I remain inside the house at all times.

"I can't bear for her to be out of my sight," he told Momma one night while wiping his red, swollen eyes. "I'm so frightened for her and for us, too. What would we do if we lost Aynnie? She's all we have left. How would we ever survive when we're half-dead already?"

One day, while he was still at home, still grieving, still waiting for the phone to ring, he saw me playing with the two tea sets that Laynnie and I had gotten for Christmas, the Blue and Pink Willow sets. Since he wouldn't even allow me to go to the backyard playhouse, Pearl had helped me set up my little table and chairs in the music room.

When he saw what I was doing, his face contorted horribly and turned almost purple. He flew into a terrible rage, out of control, yelling and sobbing. I was more frightened in that moment than I had been since my sister disappeared.

Storming over to the little table where I had set up both tea sets, he scooped up all of Laynnie's Pink Willow, carried it to the back door and threw it, piece by piece, into the street. I stood at the window and watched as each little cup and saucer was smashed into small scraps of pink and white china. With each thrust, he cried out guttural sobs that made him sound like a mad man, and I suppose that's as fair a description as any for him on that day.

When he saw that I was watching him, that I had been a witness to the entire episode, he put his head down, quickly turned away and began to weep softly. Seeing and hearing him like that haunts me to this day.

As soon as I knew Daddy had returned to his perch near the telephone, I ran out to the street, one of the places I was not allowed to go, and I picked up two of the broken pieces of Laynnie's tea set. From that day to now, I have slept with them both under my pillow each night.

A piece of Laynnie's tea set is included with the unbroken set that belonged to me. I want you to have it because it has been such a big part of me for almost all of my life. It was not just a reminder of the tragic fate of my twin sister; it was a token of our enduring love.

The other piece of the broken Pink Willow will be buried with me after my death, as I've stipulated in my Last Will and Testament. My other half, my twin sister was taken from me far too soon, but the spirit of her always remained. Laynnie has lived in my heart every day since we were brought into this world together.

As you read this, knowing that I have now left your world, be happy that Laynnie and I are once again twin sisters, our cells and spirits connected just as we were the instant we merged as one from our mother's womb.

I might have become a morbid child unable to cope with such a tragic loss. Instead, I chose to become somewhat of a maverick, one unafraid to take risks but one who never stopped looking for the other part of me. Laynnie was the fun loving part of us that could unabashedly stand at the top of the hill stretching out both arms and yelling, "I won! I won! I'm Queen of the Hill." I became as much like her as I could.

In due time, I will tell you much more about my sister. Because every thread of her existence is embedded in my soul and there is not one thing I don't remember about her.

But for today I think I have left you with quite enough to ponder.

With love from Aynnie

Cassie

My body is shaking as I fold the letter and slip it back into the envelope. Picking up the remaining piece of the pink tea set, I hold it in the palm of my hand. It feels warm, as though it has been waiting for the touch of a human hand for a long time. Maybe it has.

As I had become accustomed to doing with the handkerchief since Aynnie told me about it in her trunk full of letters, I drop Laynnie's tea set piece into my pocket. Jumbled thoughts swirl around in my head concerning my new family including the untold stories Jake has yet to see fit to tell me.

I have been thinking more and more that I should be sharing my secret meetings with him, hoping that he, in turn, will fill in some of the blanks for me. But then I imagine how that conversation might go. What exactly would I say?

Oh, by the way Jake, I met your dead mother the other day in the attic and she's been good enough to give me the lowdown on your entire family, things like her twin sister who was kidnapped and never found. You remember her, don't you? Laynnie? I'm sure your mother must have mentioned her a time or two. Right?

My imagined conversation sounds just as crazy as I think it would sound to my husband. I hate keeping things to myself and admittedly, I feel guilty for not sharing something as dear to my heart as this. A part of me wants to tell him all about it but every time I think I've summoned up enough nerve, the phone rings, the doorbell chimes, food boils over on the stove. It's as though fate is in control of the situation, which sounds just as crazy as having daily rendezvous' in the attic with a dead mother-in-law.

The appropriate time to tell him will come soon enough I feel, and when it does, I can only hope that fate will not interfere. Meanwhile, I am busting out all over to know more about the child, Aynnie's twin sister, who disappeared one day and was never seen again.

A thought: Since her body was never found, what if she is still alive?

I speak out loud. "So what happened after she disappeared, Aynnie? I have to know."

Miss Priss squirms in my lap and yawns, opening her mouth about as wide as I have ever seen it. Curious, she looks up, expecting to find another person in the room with us, someone I am talking with. If she only knew. What on earth (or heaven) is happening to me? Even the cat thinks I'm nuts and who can blame her? Here I am, sitting on a cold attic floor talking to a dead woman I never knew. And the kicker is? I am perfectly okay with it.

I look around the attic and all of the treasures it contains. Maybe Jake doesn't think of them as such, but I do. I should, however, find some way not to haunt these nooks and crannies every time the weather takes a turn. But then again, why should I? At this point, I consider myself fully invested in this Search & Discover adventure. Besides, after reading Aynnie's letter about her kidnapped twin sister, there is no way I want to get too far away from it for long. I have to know more. I need to.

When I glance at my watch I nearly jump out of my skin. Once again the afternoon has gotten away from me and I didn't have the first inkling. I look out through the dusty attic window and watch the evening shadows sink into the roof of the house next door, the deepening nightshade just starting to ooze into the shingles like colored gel. In time, streetlights will flicker on; lamplights will peek from living room windows, and up and down the street people will return to their nests to become whole families again.

And pretty soon—much sooner than I'd like to think, Jake will stroll through the kitchen door looking forward to a hot meal that I have yet to cook. I also need to pick up the dry cleaning and hit the grocery store. We are close to being out of peanut butter, the one thing neither Jake nor I can possibly live without. Yikes! I better get cracking.

Aynnie's next installment will simply have to wait.

***

As I hurry to the kitchen, I notice the answering machine message light blinking furiously. Clicking on "play" I listen while checking out what might be in the freezer that can be defrosted in a hurry. The message is from Jake.

"Hey Sweetness!" Jake's voice booms from the machine. "Just calling to remind you that I won't be home for supper. Remember I told you about The North Carolina Bar Association dinner meeting tonight? I won't be home until at least ten, maybe even later. Depends on whether the speaker is a long-winded politician. God, I hope not. I realize my being away from you breaks your little Georgia Peach heart, but you'll just have to muddle through. I love you."

Jake's laughter echoes throughout the house before the machine clicks off.

I smile, but not at Jake's silliness. I smile because I have just been given extra time to find out more about Laynnie. The dry cleaning and grocery store can wait.

After scraping enough peanut butter from the jar to make a fairly decent PB&J, I pour myself a glass of milk and anchor it on a large tray.

Holding it securely with both hands I hurry back up the attic steps, all fourteen of them, followed closely by Miss Priss. It appears that both of us are hungry for peanut butter as well as another chapter in Aynnie McMinn's book of life.

This time, after sitting down in front of the trunk and lifting the lid, I keep my eyes open and allow my gaze to fall wherever it might. It lands on another letter, one housed in a large manila envelope. I snatch it up surprised that it weighs so little. I wonder if perhaps Aynnie forgot to put something inside of it.

But as I undo the clasp and pull out the anticipated message, I see that she has not forgotten anything. In addition to the words of explanation, she has included a tinted photograph of two young girls who look exactly alike and are even dressed in identical outfits. I know immediately that it is a photograph of Aynnie and Laynnie.

I sit all the way down on the floor in what has become my signature Gandhi position, eager to learn as much as I possibly can about the mysterious twin. It still bugs me that Jake has never mentioned his mother's sister or that she had been kidnapped. I have to believe he must not have known about her. Well, one thing is certain: Aynnie will clear up the mystery soon enough.

I am not disappointed.

CHAPTER 9

Dear Jake's Bride,

Laynnie and I were born on Valentine's Day, 1940. We were named Margaret Aynne, that's me, and my twin was named Martha Elaynne.

We were cute kids, especially to others. You know how people look at twins, triplets or quads in astonishment. Laynnie and I loved each other to pieces. We were inseparable.

Momma began dressing us exactly alike the day we drew breath. We were identical, and I have often wondered how when we were babies they were able to tell us apart, especially since we wore identical clothes.

When we got older we hated that we were trapped inside matching bodies and there was not a thing we could do about it. We fancied at least a small measure of autonomy, but people made such a fuss over us that our desire for independence was hard to acknowledge.

Mother was certainly oblivious to our plight and continued to dress us alike. When we were no longer babies she hired Mrs. Singletary, a local seamstress, to fashion our clothes.

Mrs. Singletary was a whiz at the sewing machine and we always wore beautiful outfits, even if they were carbon copies of each other. It tickled our mother to see us looking like a pair of matching mittens so Laynnie and I ultimately agreed not to make too much of a fuss about it.

But parallel names? That was an area overripe for picking, one in which we felt we could and should have a say. I vividly recall the day we brought up the subject to our parents. Lord, what a day that was. I will never forget it.

"We want to change our names." Elaynne (she was still called that at the time) blurted out one night at supper right after Daddy had carved the first slice of roast beef. He calmly passed the plate on to Momma to fill with vegetables. He acted as if he had not heard my sister.

He got busy carving the second slice of meat and then, as though Laynnie's words finally hit him, he put down the carving knife and stared at her. A stunned silence fell like a rockslide over the entire dinner table.

In a minute or so, Daddy cleared his throat; Momma cocked her head to the side. Daddy, ever formal, said to my sister, "I beg your pardon?"

My sister stared right back at him, defiance etched on her face. "I don't like my name. I want to change it from Elaynne to Laynnie. Martha

46

Elaynne O'Connor is too long and too grown-up for a little kid. And besides, nobody ever pronounces it correctly."

Any resolve I might have garnered began to melt more quickly than ice cream in July. I seriously thought about keeping my mouth shut, even going so far as to wonder if I could get by with it. Would my sister be mad at me if I kept quiet? Probably.

Daddy lifted one of his brows and formed it into the shape of a checkmark. He looked at me.

"Well, Margaret Aynne? Just how do you feel about a sister named Laynnie? And what about you? Are you thinking you would like to change your name, as well?"

"Aynnie," I mumbled, barely audible. Then I cleared my throat and in a stronger voice said, "I want y'all to call me Aynnie" I paused, suddenly scared out of my britches. "Uh, if that's all right with you and Momma."

They exchanged glances and for a moment I thought our cause was lost and in addition, that we might very well be punished for the rest of our lives. Then they surprised us both by bursting into belly laughs.

From that moment on, my sister and I had names we had chosen for ourselves. I liked the two-syllable sound for Ayn-nie, but my sister, determined to keep our identities as separate as possible, at first claimed she wanted her new name to be pronounced exactly opposite to mine.

"One syllable," she said. "Laynne, like a pathway or a small street." Later, however, she changed her mind, as she often did, and proclaimed that she didn't want her name to sound like a country road. From that point on, it was pronounced in two-syllables, just like mine.

Shortening our names wasn't much of a revolution, but we felt victorious to have won a small point in our combined need for independence. And I suppose it really was a triumph, even though some people in Bear River Falls would always think of us as a Frick and Frack, which didn't change right away, even when Laynnie disappeared. After a while, I guess they got more accustomed to thinking of me, Aynnie, as an individual, forever separate from the abducted twin.

I never got used to it, though. The other half of me was gone, and like a soldier coming home from the war with a missing limb, I was acutely aware of the part of me still missing.

With love from Aynnie

Cassie

After gazing at the Olan Mills photo of the two little girls dressed exactly alike in red checked pinafores, I reach for the half-eaten PB&J. The glass of milk has gotten too warm now to enjoy, but I pick it up and sip it anyway. Then I glance at my watch. Holy crap!

Once again time had ceased to exist for me for a while and when I look at my watch it is almost eleven p.m.

I had intended to be done in the attic by the time Jake came home from his meeting but my blunder is complete when I hear the back door open and close. I am still sitting on the floor in the attic. Yikes. I don't want Jake to find me here and I am still not sure why that is. Maybe he would laugh? Make fun of me? I don't want to deal with that. Aynnie has become my friend, my confidant, and in many ways the mother I lost so many years ago.

I hear Jake calling my name and so does Miss Priss. She springs off my lap and thumps down the fourteen wooden stairs at mach speed, her nosy nature conceding no bounds.

Grabbing the envelope, I replace the photograph of the twins alongside Aynnie's letter and quickly return them to the trunk.

Hurrying downstairs almost as fast as Miss Priss, I close the attic door. In so doing, I close out another day with my new friend, Aynnie.

"Hi, Jake," I call. "I'm upstairs. Be down in a minute." I hear the eleven o'clock news theme start up on the TV, decidedly drowning out that of Maestro Chopin. I don't hear the Jack Daniels being poured, but it's easy to imagine the sound it makes.

"You look so tired, Jake," I say after a quick kiss and a tight hug. "Want me to fix you something ... a sandwich, a glass of milk maybe?"

Jake keeps his arms around me and butts his forehead against mine. "God no. I only ate half of the Chicken Kiev that was definitely not made from scratch." He grinned. "But the crème brûlée was out of this world. Lucky for me, I was seated next to Billy Ray Jordan, whom you may recall is a diabetic. He gave me his dessert which I gobbled up like a sugar junky and I am still seriously sated."

I poke him in his tight little belly. "What happened to the diet you were going to begin this week? And I'm not so sure I like the sound of you being seriously sated."

He sighs. "With regard to the diet, tomorrow is another day, Miss Scarlett. And as for the sated bit, well 'Kome wiz me to the caazbah, m'lady and we shall discuss satisfaction in great detail."

At this exact moment, I remember that I have left my half-eaten sandwich and glass of milk in the attic. Problem: how will I get it back downstairs before the mice pig out on my Skippy Peanut Butter meal? Oh shoot. Like Jake, "I'll worry about it tomorrow because tomorrow is another day.'

Well, tomorrow finally became another day and I once more find myself seated Gandhi style in front of the trunk of treasures. Eagerly reaching inside for another chapter in Aynnie's story, I grab a rather large manila envelope. It is soft and squishy. Reaching inside, I find Raggedy Ann and Raggedy Andy. Pinned to each of their clothes is the expected letter of explanation from my mother-in-law.

CHAPTER 10

Dear Jake's Bride,

I wish I could call you Daughter instead of Jake's Bride because it is how I think of you. Jake's Bride? Too detached. My Dear too formal. Besides, I always hoped I would have a daughter of my own. It was my intention to embrace Jake's wife, when he finally found the right one, as my own child equal in every way to my feelings for Jake. Alas, I will think of you as Daughter but perhaps address you as the lovely bride of my son.

After Laynnie's death, I had no other children with whom to play and I was lonely. Had it not been for my little tea parties with Ann and Andy, I feel sure I'd have been petulant or morbid and thereby would have given my parents even more grief to endure. Instead, even through my heartache, I remained the child who was seen and not heard.

As much as I looked forward to spending afternoons with the two Raggedy's, my only friends, I was constantly reminded of the missing place at the table, the vacant chair that had once been my sister's. The hole in my heart grew bigger each day until one afternoon my overburdened soul could not stand by itself one more minute.

I began to cry. Tears I had held back for so long gushed from my eyes. I couldn't make them stop no matter what, so I buried my head in my hands and let go of my long-held sorrow. I don't know how long I sat there sobbing at that lonely little table before I heard these words:

"You mustn't cry so hard, deah girl. It will give you a sick headache, you know."

When I jerked my hands away from my face, there she was. Dixie poured pretend tea into a tiny cup and made clucking Tsk, tsk, tsk sounds.

"Who are you? And how did you get in here? I didn't hear the doorbell ring."

She looked up and smiled and it was like a thousand candles were lighting the entire room. When she told me her name was Dixie, I said okay, and that was all there was to it. Just that quickly, Dixie came into my life. Though my deep dark hole was far from filled, I had created a salve for my grieving soul, an imaginary friend who saved me from myself.

Laynnie and I had pretended to have high tea each afternoon and we thought we were doing it properly. Dixie, however, was incensed at my sloppy attempts, as she called it. Little by little she taught this poor, lonely little girl what every proper Virginia-born lass has learned by the time her tenth birthday rolls around.

For a long while, I hoped that Jake would find the love of his life and that I would become a grandmother to his little girl. I wanted to use my tea set to show my granddaughter how to pour a proper tea just like my imaginary friend had taught me.

Someday I hope that you and Jake will bring a daughter into the world. If you do, please give her my little Blue Willow tea set. She might enjoy having her parties in the playhouse like Laynnie and I did, or in the music room as I did with my make-believe friend Dixie.

I have faith that you will tell her all the things I am sharing with you. Children love to hear tales about other kids in other times. Tell her about my twin sister and my friend Dixie, and don't forget to include the Raggedy's. They, too, played a very important role in my young life.

Perhaps instead of creating an imaginary playmate, your little girl will allow me to be the one sitting in Dixie's chair at her tea parties.

With love from Aynnie

Cassie

As heart-wrenching as the last two letters have been, it is such a relief to be able to sit back and actually smile at the vision of a little girl pouring pretend tea and chatting it up with an imaginary friend of her own creation. The thought of that disparate child notwithstanding, I am in a fine mood, good enough to continue plundering in the trunk. I don't need to convince myself to keep on keeping on because I'm hooked.

This time when I dig through the depths of the trunk, I find a child's toy gun. Thinking it must have belonged to Jake when he was a kid, and imagining him all dressed up like a half-pint cowboy with white hat and boots, I can hardly wait to read all about it.

What, I wonder, made this toy important enough for Aynnie to save it and include it with all the other memorabilia in the trunk? I am all ears, uh ... all eyes, Aynnie.

CHAPTER 11

Dear Jake's Bride,

My sister and I were born and raised in this house on this hill that even today overlooks the town below.

Bear River Falls has always been a close-knit community. Although progress has a nasty habit of encroaching on many small, get-away-from-it-all towns, so far it has not found our little part of the world, at least not to any great extent.

That is not to say that the Atlanta Yuppies with their iPhones, iPods and Smart Cars are not apt to discover us at some point, probably in the near future. Perhaps by the time you are reading this, they will already have made the transition from city to town. So be it.

Our father was a lawyer, one of three in town, just as his father had been before him. I suppose we were well off, but when I was a child I never thought about it much although I intuited that we were more fortunate than a lot of people in Bear River Falls. Our granddaddy had been a shrewd businessman, as well as a good lawyer who wisely steered clear of the stock market. Many of his friends and even some of his law partners went belly up when the Depression hit. Instead of investing in Wall Street, Poppa bought property

I remember him talking about how when the Crash happened, the temperament of folks in town changed dramatically. Before 1930, Bear River Falls was a friendly and open-minded place. There were church picnics and community meetings and lots of them. Folks who were rich, poor or in-between, worked and played together and gave little or no thought to who had money and who did not.

But during the Depression years, people didn't socialize much and some even lost their faith and quit going to church on Sundays. In the old days, the McMinns family had enjoyed frequent visitors but during the Depression that pretty much stopped happening.

Generations of families often lived under one roof in those days, so it was that I grew up in this very house with our parents and grandparents. Back then, it was the normal thing to do, and is probably why there were so many large homes. Grandparents had a valid role to play in raising the children and it was a fine thing. I grew up with close ties to MaaMaa and Poppa and that is not an easy thing to find within families today.

From time to time someone came to the house and knocked on the back door. When Poppa went to see who it was, he would often find a desperately poor man needing to speak with him. Most of the time he was there to ask my grandfather for a small loan so that he could buy food for his wife and children.

Poppa was a kind soul who would have slit his wrists before turning down someone begging for his family so he never failed to give whatever he could.

I remember hearing my grandfather say how heartbreaking it was to find a proud man at his door, hat in hand. In my mind's eye, I can still see Poppa shaking his head, distressed and sad that times were so hard for so many people.

He would say, "I don't look down on that man because I would do the same thing if it meant putting food on the table for this family. We are blessed."

And we were, even on the day we were robbed at gunpoint.

Each night after finishing our evening meal our family sat around the table while Poppa ranted and raved about the disreputable Congress. He would say things like, "Somebody should take a big shovel, and one normally used for picking up manure, and scrape every one of those thugs out of Washington. They don't care about the common people. They care only about lining their own damned pockets."

MaaMaa would clear her throat. "Thomas," she'd say. "There are children present. Watch your language please."

And so it went night after night. This was before Laynnie was taken, of course, so the two of us would sit quietly and try to comprehend what our grandfather was talking about and why he was so angry when he was such a mild mannered man ordinarily.

One night smack in the middle of one of Poppa's rants, the doorbell rang. Immediately, he excused himself from the table saying that it might be someone needing to see him.

In short order, we heard raised voices and a minute or so later, Poppa came back to the dining room led by a scruffy looking man holding a gun to my grandfather's head.

Daddy jumped up immediately, but the man shouted, "Sit back down or I'll kill him."

Daddy sat.

Poppa said, "This man needs of a little money. His children have come down with Smallpox and his wife appears to have caught it as well. I told him we will be glad to help him out, but he doesn't believe me."

The man with the gun looked like he was fixing to cry. "I gotta help my family and you people sitting up here in this big house, you got money. I gotta take some of it from you. Just give me what you got so I won't have to hurt you."

Laynnie and I clung to one another like two sick kittens sidling up next to a hot brick. Momma and MaaMaa were stoic, their heads lowered as if they would just as soon not have to look at the unpleasantness.

Pearl was in the kitchen when she heard the commotion. About to come out of there to see what was going on, she stopped first to listen at the kitchen door. When she realized that we were in peril, that amazing woman tiptoed back to where she kept the iron frying pan. She grabbed it with both hands.

Circling around so that she would come up on the situation from the rear and not be seen, she walked straight up to that man with a raised frying pan and brought it down on top of his head. He crumbled into a big lump and immediately Poppa grabbed his pistol.

Laynnie and I were too scared to make a sound. Momma and MaaMaa began to talk all at once but Pearl simply stood where she was with a wide grin on her face.

"That ought to teach you to come in here with a gun and threaten my fam'ly," she said.

Daddy held the gun in his hand and shook his head sadly. "It's not even real," he said. "It's a child's toy gun."

Poppa knelt down next to the man and held his bloody head in his hands. "He's not dead, thank God. The poor man probably hasn't eaten a decent meal in who knows how long. Pearl, get a wet rag and let's clean him up some and then let's give him something to eat."

Pearl was not about to agree to something like that.

"'Scuze me, Mr. O'Connor. You mean me to call the po-leese, don't you? I'm sho' you don't want me to clean up that piece of trash."

Poppa smiled. "We're going to help him, Pearl. I don't want to hurt him any more than we already have. If you get me a wet cloth, I'll clean him up myself."

She stomped out of the room mumbling words like, white trash and no account, but in a minute or so she was back with a basin of warm water and a washrag.

I watched my grandfather bathe that filthy dirty man's face and then his bloody head. He soothed the stranger in the gentle voice normally reserved for my sister and me.

When finally the man was fully conscious again, Poppa invited him to sit down at our table and eat something. He was half-starved, we could tell, but he managed with a little help from my grandfather to sit at the table as he was asked to do. He even bowed his head and said grace over the food before he took a bite. When he'd gobbled up some ham and what was left of potato salad, Poppa put his hand on the man's arm.

"How much money do you need for your family, son? I don't keep a great deal of money here at the house, but I have a little in my pocket and my son here probably has some cash on him, too. How would you feel about the two of us pooling what we have so that we can help you out tonight? If it's medicine you need for the little ones, I will call the pharmacy right now and they will give you the drugs and charge it to my account. I don't want you to go home empty handed. How does that sound to you?"

The man stopped eating and put down his fork next to the near empty plate. He didn't look at or answer my grandfather.

I was staring at him when his first tear plopped down on top of what was left of the potato salad on his plate. Seeing that broken man sitting right there at our dining room table crying is something I will never forget.

With love from Aynnie

Cassie

My eyes fill with tears as I read the story of the toy gun and my heart fills with pride knowing that I am a member of the McMinns clan. It is a legacy of which I am very proud. What good people they were and what an incredible lesson in generosity the grandfather gave to his grandchildren that night. I feel a well of pride in my heart and quickly forget all the things that had caused me concern. I was happier to be a McMinns than I had ever been.

At supper Jake is pensive, more so than usual. Earlier in the day I put together a peach cobbler, his favorite dessert, packed tight with a neighbor's banner harvest from last summer and baking in the oven while we eat. The entire house is fragrant with the aroma of ripe peaches as if heralding Georgia's famous, soon to be eaten comfort food.

After dinner I suggest we take our dessert and coffee into the den. If something is bothering my husband, I figure he will more easily talk about it while seated in his favorite chair by a crackling fire.

"Want some vanilla ice cream on top of your cobbler," I call from the kitchen. "It is still warm enough to melt it into the next best thing to sweet cream."

He says okay and I plop a scoop of French Vanilla on top of a large portion of my home state's signature dessert, but he says nothing more until I join him by the fire. As soon as I sit down, he looks at me, puts down his spoon and clears his throat.

"Cassie, I need to know why you've been so distant lately. Is it me? Have I done something to hurt your feelings? What?"

"Distant? Me? I'm never distant or moody, Jake. I'm the proverbial Mary Sunshine. You know that. What's given you the crazy idea that I'm acting weird or whatever?"

"Well, you are acting different. So what's up, Cassie? I feel like we're out of sync, that something must have gone wrong between us. I feel it in my bones and it's making me sick."

Jake begins to do the quirky thing with his lips like he does when he's trying to figure something out. Twisting his face to one side, he nibbles mouse-like on the inside of his mouth. After a bit, he takes a deep breath and sort of holds it—his way of letting me know that he is waiting for a definitive answer.

I ask myself if this is going to be it. Has the time finally come for me to spill the beans about my attic expeditions? I am suddenly skittish, not at all confident that I'm ready to tell him, so I don't. I quickly decide to wait it out. Either a needed heart-to-heart will happen or it won't.

"Jake, I'm sorry if I've seemed distant, as you put it. I'm not sure that's the right word, though. It's more that I've been a little preoccupied lately. It's got nothing at all to do with us ... as in you and me, and certainly nothing for you to be concerned about."

"Then what? Talk to me, Cassie."

I hesitate for a moment groping for the right words to come to me and they do. In fact, they tumble out of my mouth as though it is God's truth.

"Jake, I think I'm homesick. I've been thinking about Mags and Jillie a lot lately. I so wish they would come up here for a visit. It's been months since we've gotten together and I miss them so much. They're my family, Jake, you know?"

He laughs out loud. I adore the way he laughs. In point of fact, it's the first thing that attracted me to him. If something strikes Jake as even moderately funny, he doesn't have the tools to hold back. It's as if his laughter has been simmering under the surface of his funny bone waiting for the next good reason to bubble up to the surface.

Normally, his laughter is hearty and full. It is genuine and that's what I most love about it. In addition, it's contagious and, no matter how tired or upset I might be, I always find myself laughing along with him.

However, Jake has two laughs. While the one is robust and spontaneous, the other is not as natural. There's a difference between the two and it took me a while, but I learned to distinguish them.

Although he has a smile draped across his face that makes his eyes crinkle, it is his use of the second, more tentative laugh out loud that gives me pause now.

"Are you tired of me already," he asks with a smirk. "Whatever happened to forever?"

"Oh, Jake. You know that will never happen. I'm just missing my family is all. What's wrong with that?"

"Not a thing, Cassie." He keeps looking at me, not just looking, more like staring. "Don't take this the wrong way," he says, "but pregnant women get moody and fretful sometimes. Lord knows I've heard all about it from my partners. It has something to do with hormones shifting around, they tell me." He looked at me with a question mark on his face. "Well?"

"Well what? Am I pregnant? You're kidding, right?" I laugh very loud at that—maybe a little too loud.

Jake made it clear to me almost as soon as the I Do's were said and the rice was thrown that he did not want us to start a family right away. In addition, he was ambivalent about kids, he said, and wasn't at all sure when he would be ready for fatherhood. I told him that was fine with me;

I wasn't ready to be a parent any time soon. I had to learn how to be a wife before investing in maternity clothes and baby furniture.

"Jake, darling, I'm not pregnant. Believe me, you'd be the third person to know."

"The third? Okay, let me guess who the others are. Hmmmm. You would tell our friendly, but not too friendly neighborhood bartender so he would know from the get-go not to serve you any high test for the next eight or so months. And then you would confide in your good friend, the hairdresser, of course because today's woman confides everything to the scissor wizard of her choice."

I giggle. He leaves the comfort of his recliner and comes over to where I am curled up in my favorite wing chair. Leaning down, he kisses me softly on the lips, effectively stifling my nervous laughter.

"I'm not sure I want you to be, you know. Pregnant. Not yet. We've talked about this before, Cassie, and it's not that I don't like kids or anything. But I love our life just the way it is and I think you do, too. We both know how priorities get turned around and changed once children come into the picture."

"Jake, as I've told you before, I don't think I'm ready to be a mother right now, but tell me the truth. Are you sure there's not more to you not wanting kids than you're telling me? Not a day goes by when I don't hear this big old house begging to be filled up with babies. Can't you hear it, too? It's saying that we need to think about putting little people in those unoccupied bedrooms on the second floor. It's telling us that it might be time for us to think about setting more places at the table, hanging more clothes in the empty closets and buying lots more milk."

He smiles, allowing me to indulge in my momentary fantasy.

"I think of it more like filling up those dirty clothes hampers every day and twice on Saturday," he chides before pinching my cheek. "As for me, there's nothing more to it other than the fact that I want us to have plenty of moments together, just the two of us. That's all. In due time, my sweet, the only crying you are going to hear are the screams that wakes you up at 2 a.m. and then again way before you want to climb out from underneath the comfort of your grandmother's hand-sewn quilt. Until then, maybe you should think about investing in ear plugs. That way the spooky house voices can't bug you during the day or keep you awake at night."

Jake sighs and I try to look forlorn enough so that he will feel sorry for me and begin to think maybe the poor childless woman needs a kid or two to keep her company. But he sits back down and dives in to what is left of his peach cobbler with melted ice cream now running down the sides of the bowl. His only other comment is, "Yum!"

Soon after, we settle in for the evening, he with his newspaper and I with a recently borrowed library book. I want to learn more than what I was taught in school about America's Great Depression and its devastating effects on my adopted state of North Carolina.

So the subject, at least between the two of us, is closed and waiting in the wings for some other time. Shadow thoughts, however, that Jake and I might bring a child into the world anytime in the near or distant future, linger in my mind.

Almost unconsciously, I finger the pink tea set piece I now carry in my pocket just as Aynnie did for so long. A vision takes shape in my mind of a little girl hosting an afternoon tea party with Aynnie's tea set. In my mind, she is our daughter, mine and Jake's, and I have sewn the frilly pink dress she is wearing. Our daughter's name is Aynnie Elyanne in honor of Jake's mother and her beloved twin sister.

***

The next day with those same sweet thoughts still swirling around in my head, I make my way up to the attic, close my eyes, raise the lid of the old trunk and wait for Aynnie to guide me to the item she wants me to find next.

She does not disappoint me.

Aynnie's newest presentation is housed within a tiny white box, much smaller than any I have opened so far. In fact, the large letter attached to it overshadows its container and dangles over the sides.

I slit the tape from the little box and lift the lid to find a heart-shaped pendant with an amethyst set in the middle. It is strung on a delicate platinum chain. The gold filigree surrounding the perfectly cut stone is intricately detailed and scrolled. I don't remember ever seeing anything quite like it, and have to force my eyes away long enough to read what Aynnie has written about such a lovely piece of jewelry.

CHAPTER 12

Dear Jake's Bride,

You have found the precious lavallière given to me as a tenth birthday gift by my mother and father. All three of us were still grieving for our dear Laynnie, gone for over four long years, making it impossible to celebrate my birthday without thoughts of her. By that time, both Momma and Daddy had stopped hoping she would be returned to us, but I had not. Giving up was a tough thing for them because hope was what had kept them going for such a long time.

That year, just before my birthday, Momma and Daddy came into the music room where I was practicing the piano.

"Aynnie," Momma said. "Daddy and I need to speak with you about something."

"But, Momma," I said, surprised. "I've only been practicing for fifteen minutes! You never let me stop before an hour is up."

They looked at each and smiled. "Yes, you're right. But this is a special occasion and it won't take very long. You can finish your lesson after we have our little talk. All right?"

I closed my music book and swiveled around on the bench to face them. An awkward silence filled the room for a few minutes before Daddy cleared his throat and began to speak.

"Your mother and I want to talk with you about Laynnie."

My heart nearly jumped out of my dress. It soared like a butterfly. I was breathless.

"She's back? Laynnie's come home? Where is she?" My knees were too weak to stand up so I didn't dare move from the piano bench, but I wanted to. I wanted to jump up and down and shout and cry and run outside to where I was certain my sister would be waiting. She would be grinning from ear to ear expecting a big hug.

Momma is the one who moved. With a stricken look on her face, she came over to me quickly, sat down and held me close.

"Oh, dear. Oh, my darling child. No. No, your sister is not here. That's not what we want to talk with you about. I'm so sorry to have made you think that.'

My body went limp in her arms but she held on to me tightly. All the starch drained out of me at once and I couldn't speak. Not one word would form on my lips.

Daddy came over to us then. He said, "Aynnie. Your sister is not ever coming home again, and the time has come for us to let her go. Your mother and I have been sad for such a long time and we feel that our grief at losing Laynnie has kept us distant from you. We aim to do something about that now before it's too late."

He searched Momma's face as if imploring her to help him find the right words to say.

Momma ran her smooth, long fingers slowly through my hair, over and over. She said, "What happened to Laynnie, that terrible thing, left your daddy and me so full of pain that we were numb, both of us. For over four years we have grieved almost to the point of no return. Our sorrow was that deep. But we couldn't give up hope that the bad people who took her from us would one day bring her back home. That hope, Aynnie, is what kept us going when the sorrow was so devastating we didn't think we could stand it another minute."

I looked first at her and then at Daddy.

"You're giving up on Laynnie? Are you saying there's not a chance she'll come back?"

My eyes began to sting; the tears I had only shed in the dark of night inside the privacy of my bedroom tumbled down my face. I didn't care; I let them come.

Momma held me close to her heart and cried along with me.

Daddy said, "Laynnie is gone, sweetheart, and no, she isn't coming back. Your mother and I both believe that the bad people who took her away must have ..."

At this point, his voice cracked, his words faltered. He took in a big gulp of air before continuing. "... the bad people who took her away from us must have also taken her life."

Daddy got up from where he'd been kneeling in front of Momma and me. He moved over to the window that looked out on the hill where my sister and I had been playing the day she was kidnapped. With his back to Momma and me, he said, "We are a family of three now and we have to go forward, not backward. We can never, ever forget our Laynnie and I can promise you, Aynnie, we won't."

He turned to look at me. 'Thank God we still have you, Aynnie. You are our wonderful child and you are so loved. It is time to put the past behind us so that all of us can become whole again. A whole family. You, your mother and me."

I was ten-years-old. Well, almost - my birthday was two days away. It is interesting to me as I write about it now, that I understood perfectly what my parents were saying and why. I knew they were right, that it was crucial to put our grief behind us if we were to survive as a family. I marvel now that a ten-year-old was able to comprehend such an adult concept. I somehow knew that Daddy was right, and that Laynnie was gone and that I would never see her again in this lifetime. I still didn't want to believe it.

That same day, I was given the lavallière, the one I have left for you in the little white box. It was an early birthday gift given to me, I think, to bolster my feelings for the upcoming anniversary of the day Laynnie and I were born. Daddy opened the clasp and put it around my neck himself, and then he locked it in place where it has remained until today. I never took it off. Not even once.

My father gave me the necklace with his eyes squeezed shut. With them still closed he said, "Now we are a whole family again."

Having lived for as long as I have at this point, I realize now more than ever the need we all have for a sense of family.

You may wonder, and rightly so, why I have chosen to take the necklace off at this time.

It's simple, really. I have reached the point in my life where I am obliged to close some doors in order to open others. I was diagnosed with Chronic Lymphocytic Leukemia two years ago, and while I had few symptoms at first other than feeling more tired than usual, the past year has been a living hell.

Having gone through days, weeks and months of chemotherapy with the hope of a reprieve, I have finally made the decision on my own to go no further with treatment. I wasn't responding and my doctor agreed that perhaps it was time to put my affairs in order. So that's what I'm doing. Hence, the attic full of saved stuff—the history of me, Aynnie O'Connor McMinns.

I could have gone the genealogy route like many of my friends have done lately, but honestly, I think all that research would kill me faster than leukemia. Maybe you feel the same, which is why I've concocted this so-called visual history. That, plus the fact that I very much want to leave you with some tangible memories.

All of the things I've put together for you are about the O'Connor's as well as the McMinns. As I mentioned earlier, you may think it's all junk, but I don't.

So! Now that you have found the lavallière I put in the little white box, it would make me deliriously happy to think that you would ask my son to place it around your neck. My hope is that you and Jake will someday have a daughter of your own, and maybe on her tenth birthday, you will give her this necklace. Tell her it is from Granny Aynnie. I like the sound of that!

Each time I place another item in the trunk with you in mind, I feel that our bond has grown even more. Although we never met (that I know of), my heart is convinced that you and I are as one because we share something very special—love for our Jake.

With love from Aynnie

Cassie

I gaze with pleasure at what has been bequeathed to me by a mother I never met. I am so moved by her generous spirit that I feel linked to her for life. It is a beautiful feeling.

Jake! Well, there is no putting it off any longer. I have to confide in him now so that he can put the lavallière around my neck just as his mother requested. Not only do I need to tell him what has been going on but he needs to know, whether he laughs at me or not. The wonderful letters and things that Aynnie has left for us are much too precious for me to hoard as I have been doing from the start. Isn't marriage supposed to be about honesty and sharing? I have fallen short of both lately and Jake and I need to become whole again.

With each passing day I discover that my perspective on life, things I took for granted all my days, is shifting at mach speed. Even my feelings for Jake have shifted. Establishing a bond with Aynnie, as ethereal as it is, has given me a rightful place in the McMinns family. The surprise bonus of it is that I feel myself falling even more in love with my husband.

I promise myself to tell him everything in hopes that after hearing it, he will be more open to talking about starting a family of our own. First, a daughter. I will give Jake a daughter to love and cherish and worry about, and her name will be Aynnie Elaynne. Oh yes.

Miss Priss gets up and follows me to the door, quickly darting down the 14 steps in order to arrive at the bottom before I do. What a control freak she is. My footsteps are light and almost match hers as I dash downstairs to start dinner. If it were possible I'm convinced Miss Priss would have raised her front paws, stuck out her tongue and yelled, "I won! I won!!" As it is, her constant meows yell out three things: she knows what time it is, she is starving to death and she is in no mood to wait for a trifling dab of Fancy Feast.

I get Miss Priss fed, if not totally satisfied, and then prepare lamb chops for Jake to throw on the grill when he gets home. I wrap potatoes in foil and pop them in the oven, mix a beautiful salad and just as I am uncorking a nice Oregon Pinot Gris, the garage door opens and I hear the sound of Jake's car pulling in.

One glance at his stressed-out face turns me into Chicken Little. The sky has obviously fallen and my courage to fess up along with it. Once again it seems fate is intervening by shouting the message loud and clear:

This is not the time to tell him.

I smile warmly and greet him with a hug and kiss.

"Hey there, handsome. Glad you're home. I missed you today."

He holds onto me as if drawing energy from my good mood.

"Bad day," I ask, already knowing what the answer will be.

He rolls his eyes. "The absolute worst. You don't want to know. Oh great. I see you have already opened the wine. Timing, as a wise ass watchmaker once said, is everything."

"I thought we'd have these lovely lamb chops for dinner if you feel up to grilling them outside. If not, I can broil them in the oven."

He takes a deep breath and lets it out slowly, blowing pent up air out through pursed lips. "Honey, cook them in the oven tonight, if it's not too much trouble and if you don't mind. I've got a killer headache and I've also got a shitload of work to do tonight. That big trial starts in three days and two of my paralegals are out with a stomach virus. I just pray I don't get it too. You won't believe the circus it was in the office today. Talk about timing, or lack thereof."

He disappears into his study with a full glass of wine and works on his laptop until I call him for supper. Jake is quiet during the meal as he often is when an impending trial is the main thing on his mind. This one, he told me the other night, is important for him, as well as the firm. What had started out as a civil suit quickly turned into a criminal case, but if everything goes the way they hope, it will set some precedents and the firm will be appropriately compensated.

Later in the evening, after cleaning up the supper dishes and playing with the cat for a little while, I kiss the top of Jake's head, the one that is still buried in a brief.

"I'm going to bed, Sweetie. Don't stay up late, okay? Tomorrow, as the ghost of Miz Scarlett has been heard to say, and what we Georgia Peaches are too often apt to repeat ad nauseum, is another day."

He mumbles, "Fat lot that crazy bitch knew about anything."

Ignoring his jibe at Georgia's proclaimed Queen of the South, Miss Priss and I gather our dignity and go upstairs to bed.

**

Two weeks go by before I find myself sitting on the attic floor pulling things out of the trunk again. It is the morning following Valentine's Day, which is impossible for me to ignore since it was the O'Connor twins shared birthday. I made a point of not going to the attic on the 14th or the day after. I am unsure if I am ready to open up more secrets living inside the trunk.

I think about my attic visits all the time now and keep asking myself whether I need to spread them out or take them all in one fell swoop, as my momma often said. Having stumbled onto the extraordinary, something I could never have dreamed up on my own, I wonder if I should give myself more time in between to digest everything I have learned.

No matter how long I make myself stay away, there is no doubt in my mind that I will return at some point to relish every minute spent alone with Aynnie. Still I ask myself if I should wait for the days when the weather is too fowl to do anything else or my mood is equally rotten. Spreading things out could be what I need to do before I get addicted.

The handkerchief found in the trunk at the beginning of my attic visits was only the tip of the Aynnie McMinns history lessons. So far, the trunk has been filled with her memorabilia, keepsakes and stories. Everything I have found has been amazing. I remember that first day when I looked around the attic and saw all the boy stuff and then later when I found all the notes Aynnie had attached to almost everything up here. There is much more to discover and something tells me the surface has not a scratch or a dent.

Although I know it would be best to share my so-called secret life with Jake, I am still uncomfortable doing so. What I feel is warily protective of my discoveries. I know he would call me a silly goose or that would cast a negative spin on everything. Either that or he would get angry and call someone to come clean out the attic before I could do anything to stop him. I certainly don't want that. Hasn't he made his feelings about the attic perfectly clear?

The secret I most cherish is that I have become someone's daughter and I revel in my pretend adoption. I still want to learn, piece by little piece, everything there is to know about the woman who loved violets and what better place than the attic chock full of so many things that were important to her.

I feel strongly that my trips to the attic must remain an adventure just between Aynnie and me until the right time presents itself to let Jake in on my secret rendezvous'.

Oh, what the hell. Who am I kidding? I might as well give it another shot because that's really what I am itching to do. All this self-talk about putting it off is nonsense. I am determined to follow through to the end with what Aynnie and I have begun together and I'm not going to let anything thwart my efforts. I may have overdosed on Aynnie's history a few weeks ago, but I have a long way to go before I can claim bragging rights about kicking the habit.

CHAPTER 13

*Little girls learning in a little house
how to be big girls in a big house.*

Dear Jake's Bride,

Enclosed is a photograph of the playhouse Laynnie and I so loved, the place that became our second home. It's only a sweet memory now because for a long time after she was kidnapped, I was not even allowed to go in there. By the time the ban was lifted, I had all but grown out of it. Not having Laynnie there to share it with me made a huge difference. By the time I began edging toward teenagedom, I had almost stopped going there completely.

I often wonder if fathers still build playhouses for their little girls, and if they do, do their children still hold pretend tea parties in that special place like my sister and I did? I hope so. Even today, little girls need to sing lullabies to their baby dolls while sitting on the steps of their make-believe world. They need to have sleepovers rife with ghost stories and scary noises during the night. It is a girl's rite of passage, a natural part of growing into motherhood, necessary I think, for healthy creative development and social expression.

When I was young, playhouses were not unusual. My friends and I sometimes reminisce about the special times we spent in them while we were young. It was a time of imaginative worlds; funny, scary, impossible dreams, spun from a child's minds, daydreams that came to life within the tiny walls of pretend—a world apart from the real world.

The playhouse that was built for Laynnie and me turned out to be a refuge for those who followed us as well. Jake used it as a clubhouse when he was growing up. Gosh, I could have been inducted into the chocolate brownie hall of fame for all the brownies and cookies I took out there to Jake and his buddies.

They had a secret password that I, of course, was never privy to, so I would have to yell very loud: "Brownies on the porch!" and then leave. Quickly. God forbid I was ever actually seen by any one member of the group.

Before Jake took it over, my mother adopted the little house as her special place. Several years after I grew out of the playhouse, Momma transformed it into a potting shed and gardening center for her African Violets and lilacs. Slowly she began to devote what little emotional energy she had left into breathing new life into the flowers to which she had chosen to align herself. She referred to the playhouse as Mary's Sanctuary.

At the time, I didn't grasp the parallel between the short life of her daughter and that of a lilac or a violet, both of which are delicate flowers. It is obvious to me, especially now having lost a child of my own. I have always heard that we can never fully understand the enormity of a personal tragedy unless or until we have experienced a similar event. My mother used to say, "If you live long enough, you are bound to feel sorrow like you have never known before." She was right about many things, my mother, and especially so about that.

Like mother, like daughter is the phrase that ran through my own mind so often after she passed the lilac and African Violet torch to me. Only then did I begin to raise the amethyst colored flowers myself. Before I knew it, I was spending more time each day out in Mary's Sanctuary than I had since I was a little girl.

Inside that small world, I found the solace that had eluded me for such a long time. I sought and discovered new life in the delicate blooms much like my mother had done before me. It was out there in my old playhouse, that I understood why she had chosen to heal her abysmal grief inside that small world of her own making. By then, the concept was not so difficult to grasp since I had begun to do exactly the same thing. But I'm getting ahead of myself.

In my reverie, it looks like I've done what older people are so good at ... reliving their childhood. You know by now that throughout my life, I've carried my twin sister in my heart and soul, never having allowed myself to believe she was gone for good. Even today, I refuse to think of her as having been murdered. Not letting go is how I coped with her disappearance, but I will be the first to say that it is not always the best approach when dealing with tragedy. I didn't know how else to contend with the hard fact that Laynnie was no longer in my life.

The time came when the lesson I needed to learn about letting go came at me so hard I could no longer sweep it out the door and hope for the best. The thing that has worried me for a long time, however, is that my sweet Jake may never have learned that lesson. He has held onto something painful for too long a time and he needs to let it go.

At some point in your discovery, you will uncover a scrapbook with the name KEVIN SHAUN McMINNS imprinted on the front cover and you will naturally wonder about his place in the family. Kevin was my youngest son. But here I go again, getting ahead of myself.

Till our next meeting, dear wife of my oldest son, I remain ... Aynnie

Cassie

The massive attic room is shadowed by night, its wraithlike milieu embellished only by the track lighting that ekes out from the inside of what I now call 'the trunk room." Gazing out the far window, I watch as a puff of wind lifts a few dried leaves into the air. As though performing a pirouette, the leaves float for a moment before sailing downward in a soft spiral.

Folding Aynnie's playhouse letter, I put it with the photograph and place them both back in the trunk near the top before closing the lid. Bewilderment, profoundly deep, almost physically painful, attacks me. At once, I am filled with unasked and unanswered questions so intense it makes my head hurt. Hot tears for what I do not understand, spill from my eyes.

Aynnie was right; Jake has never even mentioned a brother and certainly not a word about his death. Why is that, I ask myself? Jake has been privy to all of the anguish and despair I have carried in my heart since my parents' untimely death. I cannot count the many times he held and comforted me while I carried on at the unfairness of them to be cheated out of their "dream" vacation after planning it for so long. He listened so many times as I repeated how I learned of their deaths from an offhand glance at a television set in the teachers lounge at school. How often since he's known me has he been awakened in the middle of the night because of my recurring nightmares vis-à-vis their terrified last moments? From the beginning of our relationship he has had ample opportunities to tell me about Kevin, but he didn't.

One word shouts much too loudly inside my head: secrets.

Okay, everybody has them. Even me. Have I not been the one to conceal my all too frequent attic raids? Have I not opted not to tell Jake about the bond I feel with his dead mother?

Those recurring thoughts so often make me wonder if what I am doing is not a good thing and definitely unhealthy for our relationship. I so love all the hours I spend delving into the history of Jake's family. It is far away from my normal, every day life and it definitely adds to the allure. Each day I convince myself that everything I learn will make our relationship broader, and I still think it can be. But not like this. Not keeping it all to myself, hoarding it as though it needs my protection when the only thing I have been shielding is my pride as well as the fear that Jake will somehow put an end to my trips to the attic.

I wonder if Jake somehow feels responsible for his brother's death after all these years. I do not yet know the details of how Kevin died, but Aynnie has made a point of saying that Jake was always protective. If he's feeling guilty, how he must be hurting and I need to find a way to help him open up and deal with whatever is going on once and for all. Maybe that is why I am involved in this thing. If so, I wish someone had given me a heads up. It would have been helpful if I'd been prepared for the pervading sadness shadowing this family. First Laynnie, and then apparently, Kevin.

I wake up Miss Priss who is most unhappy about it, put her on the floor next to me and watch as she routinely stretches the kinks out of her sinewy body. Then, taking a cure from her, I get up and stretch my own body in much the same way.

"Come with me, Priss, this is the day we are going for the way overdue reality check. Let's go downstairs and see what's what."

Closing the attic door behind me, I promise Aynnie to have a come to Jesus with Jake about his family (and now mine). Jake is the love of my life and I need to know everything there is to know about him and he needs to know that I will still love him warts and all.

For my part, I will tell him all about Aynnie's trunk and what all I've discovered so far inside of it. I'll tell him how over the past month or so I have learned about his mother's past and how that knowledge created a close bond between us. I know Aynnie's future letters will tell me all about Kevin and how he died, but I would so much rather hear it from Jake's lips.

By the time I reach the kitchen, however, my resolve begins to dissolve again. What on earth makes me think I can just up and ask Jake about something he has chosen to keep to himself for the entire time we've known each other? As hungry as I am to find out what happened to his brother, the hard reality remains: it is Jake's secret, not mine. If I want him to confide in me, then I need to figure out the best way to bring up the painful subject of Kevin's death. Only then can I hope to learn what effect it has had on my husband. None of it, I decide, can or should be done without more careful thought.

Meanwhile, the four burners on top of the stove as well as a decidedly cold oven await my attention.

CHAPTER 14

Dear Jake's Bride,

Yes, it's a menu and it may be the only surviving menu from the Injunction Café in existence today. I saved it because it reminds me of one of the most unusual days I ever spent as a child. It was also one of the few times I witnessed any form of affection pass between my mother and father, which in and of itself made it a red-letter day. Now when I think about what all happened, I get tickled because of everything that converged within a one-hour period of time.

Daddy used to say everything that *could* go wrong *would* go wrong at the Injunction Café, the small diner that sat catawampus to the courthouse. Daddy ate dinner there on the occasions when he was involved in a trial. The Injunction Café was convenient and the food, most of the time, was pretty good.

Although the place burned to the ground many years ago, when it was still alive and well, a bright red sign flashed on and off in the window. "Fried Chicken Special Today," it read. It was the same sign day after day so it didn't mean squat. The Injunction Café liked to brag up their homemade food, cooked-to-order from Miss Julia Mae's secret recipe file. They did so long after Miss Julia Mae was dead and buried but it was a lie. Nobody cooked as well as she did.

When she opened the place in the early Twenties, she named it The Injunction Café because of its proximity to the courthouse and it stuck long after she went to Fried Chicken and Tomato Pie Heaven.

Although the café was just a hole in the wall, it maintained a loyal and steady following for years. Five tables and a long fountain counter were squeezed into the little bit of available space, but it never achieved the cozy feeling Miss Julia Mae originally had in mind.

Customers seated at the counter were usually the busy ones who didn't have time to sit around sopping up runny fried eggs with the bottom edge of the newspaper. They were the nine to five folks. Lawyers and/or judges and even a few legal secretaries sat more leisurely at tables since they didn't punch time clocks.

When court was in session, Miz Julia's little café hummed with a swarm of fidgety men and women in a hurry to eat and get back to whatever important legal business needed to be handled that day.

After Miss Julia Mae sold the café, it continued serving decent breakfasts and so-so lunches, but business petered out around two o'clock each afternoon. The newest owner in a long line of mortgage holders since Miss Julia Mae sold out and moved to a retirement village in Arizona, was Richard Wang. He bought the café with the idea of serving food native to his Hong Kong home.

Anastasia Smith was waiting tables the day Momma and her friend Betty Sue Babcock and I, showed up after shopping at Ivey's in Charlotte for my new school clothes. I was going into the eleventh grade when school started up again in September.

When Miss Betty Sue announced that the Injunction Café had a new owner and was specializing in Chinese food, Momma and I both said we wanted to try it if we didn't have to eat our food with chopsticks.

Anastasia sauntered up to our table and threw the order pad and pencil down in a huff and shifted her weight onto her left foot. The bunion next to her right big toe, she told us, was about to kill her and she was in no mood to stand around and wait on Momma and Miss Betty Sue to make up their minds what they wanted to eat.

"Let's drink a glass of that rice wine," Momma suggested. "What's it called, Anastasia?"

She rolled her eyes. "Saké." She spit the word out like it was on fire in her mouth.

Miss Betty Sue looked at Momma in total horror. "Need I remind you that liquor makes me splotchy?"

"Betty Sue,' Momma said, clearly aggravated at her, "one saké in a glass the size of a thimble isn't going to make you splotchy."

"Well, it just might. I got so splotchy the last time I drank blackberry wine for the gripe, I had to put ice cubes in my bath water." Anytime Miss Betty Sue argued with Momma, she tuned up her whiniest voice to a higher decimal level.

"I'll have a Coke,' I told Anastasia, hoping to relieve the tension I sensed building up in our waitress. Her bunion must have been shooting regular pains up her legs because her face was pinched something awful.

"For the love of God," Anastasia clenched her teeth together, "would the two of you make up your minds and make it snappy? Your decision will not have any effect on world peace. Drink the damned saké, Betty Sue and think of it as Sanka and it won't make you splotchy." She picked up her pad and pencil and started scribbling.

Momma lost no time telling her she wanted some saké.

Mrs. Annie Ruth Kingston earned herself a certain amount of respect around town after winning a trip to California that included a free ticket to see the Queen for a Day Show. (That was a popular show during the 1950's when television was still a baby.) While Mrs. Annie Ruth was out there in California, she went to Chinatown and ate something they called Dim Sum and she liked it so much that she went back to the same restaurant every day she was there.

As soon as she got home to Bear River Falls she let it be known to everybody who would listen that she considered herself an expert on Chinese food. "I have earned the unheralded position of an Oriental food connoisseur," she said. Her proclamation impressed a bunch of people, including my mother.

"Anastasia," Momma asked, "Do we have to eat with those chopstick things or can we use a fork?"

Anastasia rolled her eyes and sighed. "Does it look to you like I'm wearing a red silk kimono, Mary? And my feet—do they look bound up to you? We are Americans here and we cut up our food with a knife and eat it with a fork. Jesus, Mary and Joseph! I don't care if you eat it with your fingers. This is Bear River Falls, North Carolina, not Hong Kong China."

"I just asked a simple question," Momma said meekly, dragging out the last few words long enough to sound almost as whiny as her friend Betty Sue, who was still trying to decide whether saké would turn her into a raspberry.

Anastasia sighed again and when she did, a button on her skirt popped off, fell to the floor and rolled across the room to settle underneath the jukebox. I remember watching that button, fascinated, but Anastasia paid no more attention to it than she would have had it been a dust mite. If someone had asked me, I'd have said Anastasia looked like she was thinking about putting rat poison in Momma's saké.

Anastasia always had bad luck with men. The last one dumped her while passing through our town. She said since there was no use crying over spilt milk she looked for and found a job in at The Injunction Café in Bear River Falls.

Anastasia finally got our orders straight and hobbled on back to the kitchen. Momma whispered to Miss Betty Sue and me, "She is just too uppity. I say to heck with Chinese food. We've lived this long without it so we can manage one more day. Let's get out of here."

Momma was getting wadded. I recognized the signs. Instead of grabbing her pocketbook and leaving, however, she lit up a Camel cigarette and blew a mouth full of smoke up toward the ceiling fan like her mission in life was to get those blades to move faster. She had only been smoking cigarettes for about a month, and the only reason she started smoking was because she wanted to look like Bette Davis. It didn't happen.

"My daddy used to say you can't make a Yankee nothing but a

Yankee, no matter what," Miss Betty Sue said, fanning away Momma's second-hand smoke.

"I remember that your daddy was a very wise man, Betty Sue, but apparently he taught you nothing about geography. Anastasia is not a Yankee; she's from Virginia." Momma took another drag on her Camel.

"Close enough," Betty Sue said miffed.

Momma no sooner blew out her Camel smoke than the front door banged open and we were jolted into the here and now by a high-pitched voice. "Don't nobody move or I'll blow you to smithereens!"

Jellycake Washington stood in the doorway with his feet splayed and waving a shotgun around the room as though watering a lawn with a hosepipe. We were too scared to move, so his instructions were completely wasted on us.

I couldn't take my eyes off him. He had orange hair curling around his blue-black face, and he wore wire-rimmed glasses that slipped down his nose every time he swung the shotgun from side to side. He couldn't have weighed more than a hundred pounds, even with a pocket full of silver dollars, which was highly unlikely given the fact that he was in the café for the sole purpose of robbing it and everybody in it. As if the dyed orange hair didn't draw enough attention to him, he wore a school bus yellow shirt with, Property of North Carolina State Mental Asylum stenciled on both the front and the back.

If Miss Betty Sue hadn't been hell-bent on bragging to the Ladies Club about eating Chinese food, we would not have been sitting ducks for a man straight out of the cracker factory.

"Don't move," he screamed again in a high-pitched voice not long out of training pants, from the sound of it. "Dump them pocketbooks on the table," he yelled.

I felt like I might wet my pants. He moved toward the back of the café, shuffling his feet a little at a time like somebody clogging.

Momma and Miss Betty Sue dumped out nickels, dimes and quarters from their change purses, then upended both pocketbooks. Coins bounced, rolled and collided in midair with tubes of lipstick, cake mascara and sterling silver compacts. Loose face powder fell out of Momma's compact and dusted the top of our table.

Anastasia had retreated to the kitchen with our order and at the time of Jellycake's entrance, she was sitting on a footstool applying a Band-Aid to the bunion that put her in such a foul mood. She was totally unaware that Jellycake was out front holding up the place. Richard Wang had walked over to the post office earlier to pick up the mail so he was still gone. Lord only knows when our food would have arrived if Jellycake hadn't showed up when he did.

When she finished doctoring her foot, Anastasia flounced out of the kitchen and through the swinging door. When she did, she crashed into Jellycake Johnson just as he was giving the room another shotgun sweep. The gun lurched upward and went off with an ear-splitting roar, leaving a hole the size of a cantaloupe where the fan had previously been attached to the ceiling.

When it began a downward spiral, Momma and Miss Betty Sue screamed like little girls. Quick as you please, Momma shoved us both underneath the table and thank the lord she did.

Anastasia heard the gunshot and immediately fell face down on the floor. Her untimely entry that preceded the gunshot blowing the ceiling fan into the middle of next week, took Jellycake totally by surprise. He staggered, grabbed hold of the shotgun with two hands and started carrying on in that high-pitched voice again.

"Stay where you're at! I'm gonna shoot anything in this room that moves!'

Picture this, dear daughter-in-law, two grown women and a half-grown girl hiding under a table designed to seat maybe three upright people if they were skinny. My teeth started clacking and Momma like to pinched my arm off but Miss Betty Sue started reciting the Twenty-third Psalm. Tears poured down her face, making the black mascara she wore streak all the way to her chin.

"Stop it, Betty Sue," Momma hissed, "before you scare Aynnie half to death. We're not in any danger. Look where we are. We are right across the street from the courthouse, and that fool is here to rob us, not kill us. Just do like he says. Help will arrive pretty soon now and we'll be fine, so hush up, for heaven's sake."

Miss Betty Sue's face was the color of a milk-fed chicken. She looked at Momma like she had never seen her before in her entire life, and then started mumbling scripture. "Yea, though I walk through the valley of the shadow of death, I will fear no evil ..."

"Aynnie," Momma said in a voice as tight as a full-blown blister, "Don't be scared. Momma's here and nothing bad is going to happen to us. Quit clacking your teeth, honey."

By that time, Jellycake was squatting down on one knee gathering up the quarters, nickels and dimes that had rolled over to where he was. I guess he figured he could get them without letting go of the shotgun. He scooped up some coins in his left hand while pointing the gun at Anastasia, still sprawled out on the floor looking like a corpse.

"Get up from there, you," he yelled at her, waving his shotgun. "And don't try anything smart or I'll blow your head clean off. I done had me a real bad day and if I'm gonna shoot somebody, it might as well be a sassy white woman."

I looked at his face and knew without question that the man and the shirt he was wearing had both originated from the same place. He was wild-eyed crazy so I prayed real hard for the Bear River Falls Police force to charge in there blasting away with six-shooters like cowboys in the Saturday movies.

Miss Betty Sue had quit with the Twenty-third Psalm by that time and was slumped against one of the table legs staring straight ahead without blinking. Her dead white face had begun to look less like a milk-fed chicken and more like the white belly of a catfish.

"Lord help us, Mary,' she whisper-whined.

"What did you say," Momma asked without ever taking her eyes off Jellycake's shotgun.

"We're gonna die, Mary,' she sobbed. "Lord in heaven, we're gonna die right here under this table at the hands of a mental person." Then she hiccupped, which sounded to me like a cannon blast in that little room.

Out of the corner of my eye, I saw Anastasia start to crawl up very slowly from off the floor like Jellycake instructed her to do. When she got to a standing position, she brushed off her uniform, reached up and patted strands of her hair back in place.

"You just tell this sassy white woman what it is you want, and I'll see to it," she said with more composure than I ever expected to come out of her mouth.

"I want all the money in that cash register, that's what I want!"

Miss Betty Sue hiccupped.

"Well all right," Anastasia answered him like he had asked for a coffee refill.

She waltzed over to the register and pushed the No Sale key. PING! Then she reached inside and took out a skinny wad of one-dollar bills. "Is this what you want," she asked, just as pleasant as could be.

Then just like that, her eyes got narrow as slits. Her full red lips folded in and became one long straight line that stretched across the bottom of her face.

Jellycake yelled, "YEAH! Hand it over!"

She looked him right in the face and said, "Come over here and get it, you miserable piece of shit!" Then she ducked behind the counter. It looked like a magic disappearing act. One minute she was there, the next she was gone.

When she popped up again, she was holding a pistol out in front of her. I knew in my soul that Anastasia intended to spray Jellycake's brains all over the room. Poor old dead Miss Julia Mae had to have been rolling over in her grave by that time. She took such pride in keeping a clean place, don't you know.

Momma grabbed the top of my head and pushed it down to the floor and then she tried her best to curl me into the fetal position I had occupied before I was born.

When Anastasia said the "S" word, Miss Betty Sue started up with the 23rd Psalm again in between hiccups.

Suddenly, Anastasia's gun went off. Pieces of glass flew like a flock of birds all over the room and I, for one, was mighty glad Momma had stuffed me underneath the table.

Anastasia's aim wasn't any better than her social skills, which meant that she hit every window in the café, a big mirror and what was left of the ceiling fan. She didn't come close to winging Jellycake however, and that riled him even more than he was to begin with.

As soon as Anastasia ran out of bullets he squinted his eyes and hoisted the shotgun, but she had enough sense to duck under the counter. His first blast took out a row of liquor bottles on the shelf behind where Anastasia was squatting, which created another big spray of glass. That took care of the saké Mama ordered. The second shot blew the swinging kitchen door into the middle of next week.

Miss Betty Sue hiccupped and then her head flopped to one side and she slithered snake-like down the table leg while the last piece of glass floated like an autumn leaf, to the floor.

Everything got quiet. I thought Jellycake and Anastasia had killed each other, so I peeked up from where Momma was mashing my head down.

I was surprised to see Jellycake standing in the middle of the floor with his shotgun dangling from his right hand like it was a slingshot. While I watched, he started sliding down to the floor, kind of like Miss Betty Sue had done. Then he rolled himself into a great big ball of a person. I was pretty sure he was dying or maybe already dead, but then he cocked his head over to one side and started giggling. That was scary.

The front door banged open about that time and Senator Godwin, whose office was upstairs over the café, burst in huffing and puffing like a big old bullfrog.

"I demand to know who the hell shot a goddamn hole in my floor," he shouted. He looked all around and finally at Jellycake who was cackling and crowing like something out of a barnyard.

"What in the name of Gawd is going on in here?" The Senator was a fat blowhard with a voice so loud that it tended to bounce even when he was speaking in a normal tone. I was never so happy to see anybody in my whole life.

"That you making all this fuss, Jelly?" The Senator looked directly at the giggling would-be robber curled up on the floor like a possum. The Senator, like most people on the right side of the law, had known Jellycake Johnson for years. Originally, I had thought Jellycake was a Bear River Falls outsider, but he wasn't. He was just another victim of poverty and ignorance, a man who had woken up that morning and decided he couldn't stay locked up in the nut house one more day.

"Do you know what you did," the Senator yelled at Jellycake. "You blew a goddamn hole in my floor, you sonofabitch." The Senator didn't seem to want to stop squawking long enough to notice the two women and me cowering underneath a table, or Anastasia sprawled out behind the counter. But suddenly, as though a light switch came on in his head, he sensed the presence of legal voters. Only then did he stop carrying on and cursing. He looked around the room and when he saw us, his mouth dropped wide open.

There was Miss Betty Sue passed out under the table with a string of drool swimming down her chin. There was Momma squeezing the daylights out of me and mewing like a cat and there I was, so scared that my teeth clacked and sounded like a train going down the track.

Behind the Senator, it appeared everybody in town was trying to crowd through the door. Searching every face, I hoped to see Daddy somewhere in the crowd, and sure enough before long I found him. Actually, I heard him before I saw him as he politely pushed people aside in order to get through. I still don't know if he knew we were in there or if he was just curious.

"Excuse me, please ma'am," he said to a pinched-faced woman. Then to another onlooker, he said, "If I could squeeze by you? Thank you. Thank you so much."

My father was always polite to a fault.

Soon as I saw him I yelled, "Daddy! Daddy! It's me, Aynnie! And Momma.' I yelled it as loud I could which then made everybody turn and look first at me and then at Daddy. That's when the waters, as it says in the Bible, parted.

Daddy took giant steps into the room and within seconds grabbed the giggling, crazy Jellycake Johnson by the scruff of his neck, jerked him up till he was standing—well, sort of standing. He glared at Jellycake like he was fixing to kill him, which surprised the dickens out of me. He didn't even look like the man I'd always known as my father at that moment.

Twisting his head around to where Momma and me were still huddled under the table, he said, "Mary, are you and Aynnie all right? Mary? Answer me."

Momma was crying too hard to say a word and Miss Betty Sue, being out cold, was in no position to speak, obviously.

"Daddy, it's me, Aynnie. We're okay, I think. Plenty scared, but we're not shot or anything." My teeth stopped clacking the minute I saw Daddy and I took that as a good sign.

In another few minutes, some policemen rushed into the café, grabbed Jellycake away from Daddy and slapped handcuffs on him. In what seemed like no time at all, my daddy was crouched down on all fours right in front of us.

"Y'all can come on out from there now. It's all over. It's safe. Hush crying, now, Mary, everything's okay. Come on out from under the table, dear."

I was still shaking, but I scrambled out on all fours like a feral kitten. Momma wiped her eyes and Daddy held her hands and helped her out from under the table. It was a sweet show of affection and so unusual for me to see that I have never forgotten it.

He glanced at Miss Betty Sue, still sprawled out on the floor, white as the inside of a coconut. Daddy thought at first that Jellycake had shot and killed her, so he yelled for somebody to call an ambulance.

Well! That scared me out of my knickers. I was crammed underneath that table all that time with a corpse without knowing it.

Miss Betty Sue moaned and raised herself up, kind of like Lazarus in the Bible, I thought at the time. She glanced around, blinking like crazy, and then started hiccupping again.

Daddy dragged her out from under the table, put one arm around Momma and then hugged me real tight with his other one. A policeman came in to take care of Miss Betty Sue, who was babbling about the valley of the shadow of death in between hiccups like she was Jellycake's cellmate.

Senator Godwin was outside holding forth to a Bear River Falls Times and Democrat reporter while trying his best to give the impression of being a hero.

I looked up in time to see Jellycake Johnson with his hands tightly cuffed behind his back being shoved around by two supersized policemen. His head drooped down so far that his chin appeared to be resting on some of the stenciled letters of the mental asylum shirt he wore. Big drops of tears rolled down his blue-black face and in that quick minute, I felt his defeat, his utter lack of hope in my own soul as keenly as if it were my own. I had to look away.

Daddy guided us through the gawkers that continued to hang around hoping to see blood or shot-up people. When they saw us coming, they stepped aside, creating a wide path so me and Momma and Daddy could get to our car. I remember how special they made me feel.

Anastasia sashayed out the front door right after we did. I rolled down the car window so I could hear what she was saying to the newspaper reporter.

She threw her shoulders back and put a grin on her face as wide as the Mississippi River. "Hot Awmighty Damn!' she announced as if she were on stage. "I wasn't scared. I meant to pull that trigger and I'd do it again in a New York minute."

The reporter stared at her as though she needed to go to the hospital along with Jellycake Johnson. Then he shrugged his shoulders and walked away mumbling that every Yankee he ever knew was crazy as a Betsy bug. I figured it must be a common thing that North Carolinians as a whole didn't know squat about geography.

"Virginia," I mumbled to the reporter even though I knew he couldn't hear me. "She's not a Yankee. She's from Virginia."

CHAPTER 15

Dear Jake's Bride,

Ah ... now you have found my bridal photograph. It was taken a few months before the actual ceremony, although I probably looked pretty much the same on my wedding day, maybe with a little less makeup. It's hard to distinguish my coloring and features in a black and white photo, so I will tell you that I was blonde back then with green, Irish eyes and I was slender. Other than that, the photo pretty well speaks for itself although I don't look a thing like that these days.

We had a lovely noon wedding and the reception was everything a bride and groom could have hoped for. We danced and received champagne toasts (lots of those) and laughed. Oh, how we laughed. Both James and I were high on our special celebration as well as each other that day.

We met when James joined my father's law firm as an associate. After having clerked for him the summer before, Daddy was convinced that James had earned and deserved a place in the firm. I didn't meet him that summer because I was spending two months in Europe and by the time I returned, James had gone back home to Cedar Pines and then to law school in Virginia to complete his last year. He was brilliant so of course he made law review at the school founded by Thomas Jefferson. That alone placed him in high regard as far as my Daddy was concerned.

James adored my father. They had a mutual admiration club going for them from the get-go. My husband never allowed anyone but Daddy to call him Jimmy. I was never sure he was really comfortable permitting my father that particular consideration but it would never have occurred to James to tell Daddy to call him by any other name.

Before James even finished law school, Daddy offered him the associate's position. He asked James to consider coming back to Bear River Falls to work in the office while studying for the North Carolina Bar which he did and then made Daddy over the moon happy when he passed the first time. Once he confided to me that he had high hopes for James' future. I think Daddy expected him to one day take a seat on the bench and because he thought so highly of him, there was no doubt in his mind that James become a formidable jurist.

I was earning extra credits in summer school at Queens College in Charlotte at the time James formally joined the firm, and each time I came back home, all I heard was, "Jimmy this" and "Jimmy that." In my father's eyes, James McMinns was the son he never had and I knew it.

Curious and a little intrigued, I made it my business to meet this fellow about whom my father always bragged. I went down to the office one day after summer school was over and introduced myself to him and just like that, with basically one look, our future together was set in stone. The mutual attraction was like a static shock and by Thanksgiving, we were hopelessly in love and everybody was happy about it.

James gave me an engagement ring that Christmas and I hope it is the one you now wear. I specifically told Jake to have it remounted when he found the right girl. James and I got married the following June because I had always dreamed of being a June bride.

The gown I wore (the one you see in the picture), was the same one worn by my mother in 1934. Hardly any alterations were needed because Momma and I were the same size. I so adored that dress. Made of creamy satin and silk, I can still remember the feel of its cool silkiness gliding over my nubile body.

Momma insisted that I wear a girdle, but I hated the idea and I remember we had a terrible argument about it. Had it been left up to me, I'd have walked down the aisle in that satiny-silk dress without one stitch on underneath—most certainly without a girdle! Momma saw to it, of course, that I was suitably layered long before the organist began to play Handel's Water Music, the stodgy Episcopal rector's preference to Lohengrin's Bridal Chorus. The old fool was adamant that the pagan "Here Comes the Bride" would not waltz me down the aisle to my waiting groom.

Oh my lord, the buttons! My college roommate, Joanie, was my maid-of-honor and she was the one who helped me get dressed that day. Joanie could out-cuss a sailor. Well! She used up just about all the four-letter words in existence at the time while buttoning up my gown. I can hear her now.

"Goddamn buttons. Do you know how many teeny-weeny buttons are on this dress? A person needs to have midget fingers to get them all done up."

I laughed. I had to. Joanie was the only person I ever knew who could cuss all she wanted to and still sound no more obscene than if she were reciting the Gettysburg Address.

"Joanie, I don't know how many buttons are there and I don't care. Buttons are not the predominant thing on my mind on this day of all days."

She stopped fiddling with them. "Well, I counted them. Fifty-eight of the Goddamn things, not including the thousand or so on your sleeves that go all the way up to your Goddamn elbows. Hell's bells! I'm never going to get you dressed in time for the ceremony. Your guests will be eating Goddamn breakfast in the morning before I've finished with these damn buttons. You might as well tell them to go on home and come back again tomorrow. And if you think James is going to get inside this gown of yours later on tonight, you might as well forget it. He'll be an old man before he can unbutton you out of this frock."

Joanie always exaggerated because that was her way, and I loved that about her. She could make the most ordinary things come alive with her embellishments. That day, however, she was right about those fifty-eight plus buttons. It took forever to get me dressed. But when I turned around and saw myself in the full-length mirror, even I had difficulty believing I was gazing at me, Aynnie O'Connor, inside that beautiful gown.

And James—I couldn't have dreamt up a more handsome groom. I adored his thick head of sandy brown hair and those chocolate-colored eyes. All he ever needed to do that day, and for all the years that followed, was to look at me and I was lost in his eyes.

James had a square jaw and a Roman nose. Aristocratic. When I look at my Jake today, I'm swept back in time to when James was his age. Father and son look and act so much alike.

The gown, in case you might one day be interested, has been hermetically sealed inside a large box, or so I was told at the shop that specializes in the preservation of vintage clothing. I realize, of course, that you won't be wearing it since you are already married. However, there may come a day when my future granddaughter is about to become a bride and she may want to take a look. Perhaps she will even want to wear it, and if that should be the case, the gown that was passed down through the generations is hermetically available to her, along with the bridal handkerchief, if course. That, too, is also hers for the asking.

Love from Aynnie

PS:

If you would like to see the gown, the box is stored here in the attic. It is in the small bedroom closet. You can't miss it.

Cassie

It is impossible for me to read Aynnie's account of her wedding, the description of her beautiful gown and not have my own wedding day feelings overlap with hers. She showed me through her words how much in love she was with Jake's father and it took me back to the day Jake and I got married. I had almost a copycat wedding, even down to the point of having worn my mother's wedding dress too. Reading her latest letter was uncanny.

And how about her Joanie and my Jillie? If they had been cloned they could not have been more alike. Reading about her wedding gave me a huge case of déjà vu.

Oh Aynnie. We should have met before now. Wasn't it Sherlock Holmes who said something about fate being a fickle mistress? I am beginning to think it is fate, and all of its many other layers that has kept us from getting to know each other until now. When I allow myself the luxury of speculative metaphysical thinking, I can almost see you and my mother playing bridge together in the hereafter. You are both laughing and one of you is saying, "Well finally! I was beginning to think she would never figure things out! I call that a grand slam."

CHAPTER 16

Dear Jake's Bride,

The two birth certificates in this packet belong to my two sons, Jake and Kevin.

After James and I were married, we lived for over a year in a small house on Findlay Street, just a few blocks from my parents and the house where I grew up. It was an idyllic time for James and me because we were in love and so damn young! I wouldn't trade that year for anything in the world.

Our idyllic life came to an abrupt halt when my father had a massive stroke a year later. He died. After his death, I spent a lot of time with Momma who was understandably devastated. It reached the point where I was spending more time at her house than I was at my own but since I had no children yet, I didn't mind. My mother needed me so anything I could do to make things better for her was what I did.

James was snowed under trying to pull things together at the law firm, struggling hard to do what he thought Daddy would want him to do. After Daddy died he basically became head of the firm overnight. I hated leaving Momma alone in the big house especially at night, so it was no surprise to anyone when we decided to move in with her. It made sense. I was torn leaving what I had begun to think of as our honeymoon cottage, even though the prudent side of me knew it was best for us all to live under one roof.

The living arrangements actually worked out very well and especially so because after two years of marriage (more than a decent interval), I was pregnant with James, Jr.

We called him Jake almost from the day he drew breath because it suited him much better than Junior and James absolutely refused to entertain the idea of calling him Jimmy. Some of my friends who had borne sons insisted on calling them "Little John," or "Little Something Else" after the daddy, but I hated that idea as much as my husband hated the idea of Jimmy. There was no way I would ever have called him "Little James" or even worse, "Bubba." Jake was Jake from the very first day of his life.

He was a beautiful baby, fat and healthy. When the nurse brought him to me, the first thing I did was count his fingers and toes and then I did all of the other things new mothers have been known to do since the beginning of time. He was perfect and I remember thanking God for allowing James and me to create such a beautiful work of art together.

Momma lived long enough to know and enjoy her grandson. She doted on him and he ate it up. What a devoted pair they were. I have so often wished that she had been around longer, but that was not to be. She died when Jake was two-years-old.

I was pushing thirty when I gave birth to another son, Kevin. From the start, I sensed that something was not right. Kevin did not cry. While Jake had been born a healthy baby, Kevin came to us not so healthy. After years of trying to convince ourselves that he would catch up in time to other children his age, we were forced to look reality in the face.

By now you are most certainly aware that the life of a young attorney revolves around his profession. It is the nature of the beast, I'm afraid and many a lawyer's wife has had to accept a secondary position in the pecking order. In my case, since my father had been an attorney I knew what I was getting into even before we got married. Had I not seen it first hand all of my life?

From the time James and I fell in love, we enjoyed a strong bond. When he began to spend more hours in the office than he ever, I accepted it like I had been taught that a good wife should. He had his own clients to consider plus all of Daddy's leftovers he inherited. I didn't think too much about it because I had my hands full caring for the children as well as our home.

Thinking now about how the circumstances gradually developed I can look more realistically at how it all played out. It was inevitable that the threads of trust and loyalty on which we had built our marriage were destined to unravel. Distance had crept into our lives unheeded so when the first telltale sign appeared, it was a blow to me and it was incredibly sad.

I had known on some level that the gulf between us was growing; James knew it, too. Neither of us had knew how to combat it or what it would take to fix it. We both put an enormous amount of shared energy into raising our two rambunctious boys, and in addition, James had the law practice to consider. He did what he could to help me with the boys, but more often than not, raising the children and running the household was my responsibility. James happily left that part of his life up to me. Kevin demanded so much from us and I am sure it took a toll on our marriage. Even so, I am certain of one thing: James and I did the best we could with the hand of cards we were dealt.

Kevin's physical disabilities left him pretty much incapable of doing a lot of things so he was dependent on me, his primary caregiver. Jake, on the other hand was a typical little boy, curious and active. I was honestly so worn out by the end of the day that I didn't have much of anything left to give to James, either physically or emotionally. I knew in my heart that our relationship had shifted, but I convinced myself that it was temporary. All marriages go through change and ours was no different. I didn't know what to do about it or whether I should do anything at all. Even if I had known, I probably would have done what I did which was nothing. I was too damned tired.

My storybook marriage, the one I had believed was held together as tightly as those fifty-eight buttons on my wedding dress, was about to come undone, the aftermath of which would be one more devastating blow to our entire family.

The rest of the story will have to wait for another day.

Cassie

And I, Mrs. James (Jake) McMinns, Jr. will look forward to reading all that you have to say to me on another day, Aynnie. Right now, however, I have a zillion errands to run, a kitchen to stock with groceries and Miss Priss is due for an allergy shot from her least favorite person on the plant: Doctor Kate, the cat vet.

I never in my life ever heard of a cat with allergies. Aren't they the ones that are supposed to give *us* allergies? How dare they claim that function for themselves?

CHAPTER 17

Trouble, oh we got trouble,
Right here in River City!
Trouble with a capital "T" ~ Meredith Wilson

Dear Jake's Bride,

I am sure you are wondering why I bothered to include a matchbook cover from the Biltmore Bed and Breakfast Inn. You may already have guessed that it has a story to tell and as much as I don't look forward to telling it, the time has come to spit it out.

Trouble hit us the day when everything seemed to be going right.

I slipped out of bed that morning believing that all was right with the world and that nothing could possibly go wrong. Having had a good night's sleep for a change, I felt good. The children had been sick with a virus and projectile vomited all night for close to a week. Every time I fell into a half decent sleep during that week I would hear, "Momma! Momma!" Sleep is the one thing a mother never gets enough of and you can take that to the Delivery Room with you when your time comes.

When my feet hit the floor that morning, James rolled over and let out a soft snore, so instead of waking him as I normally did, I opted to let him have another few minutes of uninterrupted snoring. I would perk the coffee so that when he woke up to the aroma he loved, perhaps his day would begin on as pleasant a note as mine.

I made oatmeal for the boys and got them fed and settled down as soon as I could. Then I fried the bacon as crunchy as potato chips, somehow got the eggs to come out sunny side up the way James liked them, and I even cooked a pot of grits with nary a lump. The biscuits were light and flakey and by the time James got dressed and came downstairs, his breakfast was on the table. Even his first cup of coffee was poured and waiting for him to take a sip or a gulp depending on how quickly he needed the caffeine.

"I have never eaten a more delicious breakfast, Aynnie," he told me after diving in like he had just come off the Bataan death march and was starving. James was not the kind of man to make a fuss over meals, especially breakfast. My good day, I thought to myself, just got better and I would not allow anything to mar such a beautiful beginning.

I was so wrong.

When the phone rang later that afternoon, I answered it but didn't recognize the voice on the other end. She asked for James, inquired rather, if he might be the same James McMinns who had lived and gone to high school in Cedar Pines, a small town two hours from Bear River Falls.

"Why yes, that would be my James but he hasn't lived there for years. Are you an old friend of his from Cedar Pines?" I thought it was a reasonable question.

The feeling I had woken up with, that God was in his heaven and all was right with the world, was about to crash down on my naiveté. The blow came when she started to speak.

"An old friend," she said with an edge to her voice. "James McMinns and I are much, much more than just old friends. At one time we were planning to be married. That all went to hell in a hand basket, of course, when you and your father interfered and messed everything up."

I was stunned. Until that moment, I didn't know that James had been involved with anyone before we met. He told me that he had dated a lot of girls, but we both felt it was love at first sight for us. He never even hinted that there had ever been anyone else. Certainly, not someone to whom he had been engaged. I thought then and I think now that it should have been worth a mention, don't you? To top it off, the woman practically accused me as well as my father of stealing him out from under her. No pun intended. Well, maybe it was a little bit intended.

She said, "After James told me about you and that he planned to marry you and live in Bear River Falls, I was so heartbroken that I married another man for pure spite. It was a bad decision made on the rebound because it didn't work out. How could it? He wasn't James, and James was the only man I ever loved and the only man I will ever love."

I asked if she and her former husband had children. She told me they did.

"Three," she said. "Two boys and a girl. They are good kids and they stuck by me throughout the terrible ordeal with their father. Through thick and thin, you might say. Believe me, there was a lot more of the thin than there was of the thick."

Her laugh was as bitter as alum.

I didn't respond to her. Everything she talked about came at such an unexpected moment. It was the last thing I ever thought I would hear, and I never expected to be the recipient of such news over the telephone. I wanted to hang up and return to the beautiful day I had been given before 3:07 p.m. Eastern Standard Time, but something inside of me told me not to do that.

After a long enough pause on her part as well as my own, I cleared my throat. "I'm sure James will be disappointed to have missed your call, Mrs ..."

"Just tell him Tommie Sue called to say hey," she said, sounding possessive and at the same time dismissive as if she were giving orders to a servant.

I was about to take her to task about that attitude of hers, but before I could say another thing, Jake let out a scream that sent chills down to my toenails. I slammed down the phone and ran to where the boys had been playing with toy soldiers when the phone rang.

When I got there, Jake was still screaming. He was holding his head as though trying to keep it from toppling off his neck.

"Kebin hit me with de twuck," he said over and over. What an understatement that was. Jake was sporting a goose egg the size of a golf ball.

Later, after I calmed him down and put ice on his forehead, both boys were ready for a nap, thank goodness. I began to read a story to them but they conked out before I could finish. Jake fell asleep so quickly that I was concerned about a possible concussion because of that goose egg, so I called our doctor who told me to watch him closely. He might just as well have said, 'give him two aspirin and call me tomorrow'.

I was overwhelmed. The feeling of unease and uncertainty in every area of my life began a slow crawl up to my brain. It was as though the summer humidity had suddenly spiked to the point that the air was as thick as a mud pie making it hard to breathe. I wondered, silly as it sounds now, if I was having a heart attack. Surely not. I was only thirty-two-years-old.

A remembered sentence grabbed my brain: *the wife is always the last to know*. If I'd heard it said once, I had heard it a hundred times. Was that what was happening? Was my mind beginning to wrap around something I had been keeping at bay, pretending not to know?

Tommie Sue's voice echoed in my head as though I were still hearing her words and how they had been delivered all over again. I heard the condescension and I am now positive that she did it on purpose with the hope of making me feel inferior to her. Oh, she was full of guile, that one, as I was to find out later. Much later.

When I met her a year after that phone call and looked into her face, I knew without a doubt that she had planned and executed her involvement with my husband from the beginning.

By that time unfortunately, it was almost too late for any of us. The damage was done to our storybook marriage and could not be undone.

Cassie

Once again I sit perfectly still in my usual position: cross-legged on the floor in front of the open trunk. My mouth is open in astonishment but my mind is anything but still. After reading all about the perfect wedding, the perfect wedding gown, the perfect wedding reception — all of which was followed by the perfect marriage and the blessing of a perfect child, I am stunned to read the unraveling account of it all.

I am torn. Truth be told, I am not sure if I want to know any more details or if I would rather close the lid on the trunk, take my cat and me downstairs and never hoof it up those 14 steps again. I get back to the life I put on hold, the life that holds no secrets at all. Well, maybe one or two but nothing like what is contained in a matchbook cover.

Or I can do the thing Aynnie wants me to do, what I think she hopes I will do. I can learn all there is to know about this family to which I have become a part. I can learn to love them, living and dead, warts and all.

I have a feeling that the next letter will go to the heart of Aynnie's life as a wife and as a mother and she will tell me more about Jake's brother, Kevin. I am left with no real choice but to delve into what she is offering as deeply as I dare.

Do I dare?

CHAPTER 18

"You'll tell yourself anything you have to,
to pretend you're still the one in control." — *Jodi Picoult*

Dear Jake's Bride,

You must be wondering why I included an empty bottle of Mister Bubble in my trunk of memories. Well, it is a simple explanation.

When James came home the evening after the ominous phone call from his old girlfriend, he was even later than usual. The both boys were in the bathtub and I was on my knees on the cold tile floor trying to keep Kevin still long enough to get him clean. James walked into the bathroom as soon as he heard the boys laughing and squealing as only two little brothers can do.

"Well, there you are, my family," he said as though we had just that minute turned up in the Lost and Found at Ivy's Department Store in Asheville.

Jake, who was born with an immeasurable adoration for his father, beamed like the morning sun had walked into the room to shine only on he and his brother.

"Daddy! Look at my goose ball." Peacock proud, Jake stood up, naked as a jaybird and turned his face up for James to admire his most recent war wound, courtesy of brother Kevin.

James frowned but quickly covered it with a half-smile. "A goose ball, huh? Looks more like a baseball to me. Kevin must love you a whole lot to give you a big old baseball, Jake."

I had not said one word to James, nor had he acknowledged me. Kevin, bless his dear little heart, kept splashing the water with his hands. He felt no guilt whatsoever for having been the cause of Jake's "goose ball," and for that I was glad.

"It's called a goose egg, Jake," I said. "But I think yours is almost the size of a baseball. Don't you think so?"

He patted his newest attention-getter with affection, grinning all the while. "Jake likes goose ball better. Jake not like eggs."

James stooped down beside me then. "How did you let this happen?" It could have just been my mood but it seemed to me that his question was more accusation than concern. I was totally out of patience by then and tired beyond belief. Cranky. The fact that my husband had come home late once again revived my insecure feelings that began with Tommie Sue's phone call. I put down the washcloth and soap and turned to face my husband.

"You ask how I could let this happen? Well, let me see. Was it their first altercation of the day or was it the fiftieth? Silly me, I just can't seem to keep their skirmishes numbered sequentially. I do remember leaving them for a very, very short period of time in order to answer the telephone. And yes, I do believe that while I was having a one-way conversation with a woman named Tommie Sue claiming to be your former fiancé, Kevin bonked Jake in the head with his new toy truck. Jake screamed like a hyena, bled like a stuck pig, but I managed to handle the situation. Is that clear enough for you, Counselor?"

Until that moment, I had not realized how angry I was with him. When did that happen and why had it come out at that moment? I suppose it had been building up. Either that, or I had become a jealous wife cliché that very night and all because of one asinine woman who had the temerity to phone my husband at our home.

I could understand my indignation over that one morsel, but why had I become so angry with James who, as far as I knew had done nothing to deserve it? Nothing except to keep Tommie Sue Somebody a secret from me. Tommie Sue Somebody who, according to her, he had once loved and promised to marry.

Well, I ended up doing what I always do when my emotions go haywire. I cried. Not just a little bit. I really carried on. The boys had never seen me like that and it scared the bejesus out of both of them. They started bawling and howling and before I knew it, that little bathroom could have been renamed the incorporated town of Coocooville.

You may be wondering how James reacted when the chaos began to swell. He walked out of the room and left the family he had only recently fished out of Ivy's Lost & Found.

The day that had started out so perfectly ended up being one of the worst in the history of Aynnie McMinns. That is not to say that it was THE worst because there were other rip-snorting bad times ahead that I could not have anticipated that particular day.

It was the start of an awfully bad time for James and me. Days that followed often made me wonder how on earth our relationship could possibly survive. A lot more happened in the months ahead, but right now I don't feel up to going into it. Even after all these years and everything that has happened since, it still upsets me to remember those bad times.

We made it. I think we did because we are good people. I am a firm believer that strength comes to those who look at trouble in the face and handle it when pushing it away would be so much easier.

You are Jake's wife and you are as much of a McMinns as I ever was. Since the day you walked up the 14 steps to the attic, opened the trunk and reached this point in my self-styled memoir, you are invested. You deserve to know all there is to know.

I promise to tell you everything in due time, my dear.

Aynnie

Cassie

I feel torn up inside and full of the same kind of agony and confusion Aynnie must have experienced. Her feelings of betrayal and abandonment must have been so significant and as hard as it is to learn of it, I'm glad she chose to tell me all about it.

I can picture the boys playing and splashing each other in the bathtub but I can also feel the weariness she was feeling but did not put down on paper. Her utter shock at hearing a voice from James's past must have thrown her for a loop. I got it. If one of Jake's old girlfriends called him on the phone and I happened to be the designated message taker, I would have been livid.

The despair that Aynnie felt in every corner of her world came through loud and clear in her letter and I wished—not for the first time—that she and I had met before that became impossible. I would have listened as she told me her life stories and there is no doubt in my mind that we would have become friends. Close friends.

CHAPTER 19

Dear Jake's Bride,

If I were seated next to you right now I would love seeing that you are holding what you have to think is the strangest picture you could ever have found in this trunk!

That said, I'll add to one other thing: it is the best visual I can find up to explain how my son and I began to see the world so differently, perceptions that throughout Jake's life have too often kept us emotionally separated.

A great deal of what I find myself doing these days is looking back on the life I had as well as the life I could have had, and I wonder if my need to be true to myself was worth the distance it so often created between a mother and her child.

I love my son, but I am not sure that he has always felt loving towards me. Most certainly, love has not always shown up as a shared feeling between us. For many years I agonized over the disparity and tried so hard to understand what had happened. It took me a long time to figure it out, and even now I'm not totally convinced that what I think I know is correct.

Jake wanted me to be a copycat mother, one who looked and cooked like Betty Crocker. (In today's world it would be Martha Stewart or Rachel Ray). He would have been happier with me had I been more stereotypical, if I had taught Sunday school, been a Cub Scout leader and brought cookies to his schoolroom once a month.

Jake was unable to see and certainly didn't appreciate that I could never have been what he wanted me to be. There's nothing wrong with women who choose a more traditional role than I did, but it just wasn't my thing. It didn't fit me and that embarrassed Jake.

One time when Jake was in third grade I was asked to bring cookies to his classroom. The teacher was having a big birthday party for all the summer kids who didn't get to celebrate their special day during the school year. She asked several mothers to contribute sweets and Kool-aid for the party and I happened to be one of them.

I was happy to do it but because I've never done anything the normal way, I decided chocolate coconut and pecan cookies shaped like a big foot would be fun for the kids. I didn't bake them. I went to the local bakery and together we came up with the idea of a kooky cookie.

It was so much fun. Not only did the cookies taste great, they looked as much like a big old gorilla foot as is possible when dealing with flour, sugar, nuts and coconut. When I saw the finished product it gave me another idea. I rented a hairy gorilla suit and delivered the foot shaped cookies while wearing the costume.

The kids loved it. They squealed and giggled and laughed like crazy while trying to figure out who was inside that costume. Well, most of the kids loved it; Jake was not one of them. He quickly figured out who the gorilla really was and needless to say, he was not amused nor was he a happy camper.

"Why couldn't you just bring plain old sugar cookies like a normal person," he shouted that night before storming upstairs to his room. He even refused to come down for supper. The next morning he got up early, ate a bowl of cold cereal and then rode his bike to school before I even got out of bed. Clearly, he was embarrassed to claim me as his mother.

I tried talking with him about it later, but as you probably know by now, Jake can be the king of remote when an uncomfortable situation confronts him. After a while and a lot of tears I stopped trying to explain myself and I stopped feeling bad about the gorilla episode, too. Instead, I made a point of remembering the happy faces on the other young students.

I created a light-hearted memory that day for all of the children with the exception of my own. It turned into a bad memory for him, compliments of his own mother and one in which I was never able to revise.

I love Jake to pieces but I so wish he could learn to lighten up. His serious nature reminds me so much of his father. If you ask me, James too often behaved like an English barrister, staid and proper at all times. In fact, he was a carbon copy of my own father. I suppose maybe that's why I was attracted to him in the first place. He was so like Daddy that it was immediately comfortable for me to be around him. Such a good man James was, and regardless of his stoicism at times, there is no doubt that he loved his family, every one of us, in his own way.

Sometimes I think perhaps James's need to be proper was a gene passed on down to my Jake, along with the lawyer gene. It wouldn't hurt Jake one bit even now to learn how to more easily relax, to bust out laughing every now and then. I hope you will be the one to bring out the lighter side of my son one of these days. I know it is in there somewhere because I remember the wonderful laughter that bubbled up from him when he was a boy.

If you are able to accomplish this, then there is hope that he will begin to think of me in a more loving way than he has done in the past. Maybe then our distinct personality differences will be a happy bond that existed between us and not an embarrassment. I have a feeling that I will not live to see that happen but who knows? Maybe I will be looking from some other dimension and when that happens, I will smile and thank you for making it happen.

Cassie

I fold the letter and place the gorilla photo and the smaller one of the third grader group next to it. After what I have learned lately, it doesn't surprise me that Jake never mentioned the incident or much of anything about his parents. When I ask about either one of them, his answers are invariably short and factual as though he is a coached witness testifying in a big trial.

One thing I know for certain. Aynnie is right about my need to draw Jake out and to help him relax. His lighter is one I've seen on occasion and it's always delighted me. But that's just it. His serious side too often defines him.

I need to figure out a way to get him talking about his mother, his father and that dear brother of his. He needs to do that because he needs to have faith that I will understand. Now that I am privy to his mother's perspective I want to know his family from his point of view.

Oh, Aynnie. You certainly know how to push my buttons!

CHAPTER 20

Dear Jake's Bride,

The little teddy bear you are holding was named Boo Bear. It belonged to Kevin and it was his constant companion. It was given to him, to us really, the day he came into the world. That was before we ever suspected anything might be seriously wrong with our boy.

Looking back, as I am prone to do more and more these days, I can easily identify the unsettling feelings I carried with me from the first time I held Kevin in my arms. I didn't know then what to look for, but when a newborn baby never cries, it sends up alarm signals, or it certainly should. I noticed, but reluctantly acknowledged that Kevin was not as responsive as Jake had been at the same age. Not only did he not cry but also he made no baby noises at all. No goo-goo sounds or anything like that. Had I been more enlightened, however, I would have watched for signs like Kevin's inability to make eye contact. In trying to convince myself that all mothers engage in abnormal fears when it comes to their young, I shook off my bad feelings when I should have been paying attention.

I remember when four-year-old Jake came flying out of the front door to greet us the day we brought little Kevin and Boo Bear home from the hospital. Jake took one look at that baby and his face showed an immediate, total and complete love for his new brother. I had never seen anything like it in the child.

I often went to the nursery and found Jake standing by Kevin's cradle rocking it gently while the baby slept. More than once I saw a tear or two fall from Jake's eyes.

When Kevin smiled for the first time, Jake was the one who stood next to him chattering baby talk and giggling. Okay, so the baby was expelling gas; I choose to think otherwise.

From the get-go, it was as if Jake was Kevin's self-appointed protector and I found out later that nothing could ever change that. Their bond grew in direct proportion to their ages. It was a beautiful thing to watch, this simple adoration between two brothers.

Even so, Kevin was a handful. He demanded so much of my time and if it had not been for Jake, I would not have had a minute's rest. It was true that at first Baby Kevin did not cry, but later when he found his cry button he pushed it for hours at a time. He also screamed a lot.

Doctor Johnson examined him so often I'm sure he thought of me as an overprotective nutmother. I would give the doctor a complete rundown of Kevin's behavior, his constant screaming, his inability to connect with anyone but Jake. Then I would ask, "Is my baby hurting? There must be a reason why he cries all the time. How can I help him?"

Dr. Johnson was a good man but he didn't think there was any need to perform tests on my little boy. "He's a colicky baby, Aynnie. He'll get over it and so will you."

But that's not what happened.

The only time Kevin did not scream was if Jake was by his side soothing him with sweet, gentle words. The thing is, it wasn't Jake's job to take care of Kevin; it was mine. Lord knows without those few minutes of peace and quiet Jake managed to coerce from his little brother, I feel sure I would have had a breakdown.

When Jake started school he got involved with Scouts and softball and all kinds of activities and it followed him from grade to grade. After school, he had homework to do or softball or some other kind of practice. That left Kevin and me by ourselves all day long with little or no relief in sight.

My friends were great, so supportive. They made themselves available so that Jake would always have a ride to afterschool activities at such times when it was impossible for me to take him myself. Occasionally, I would say to hell with it, put Kev in the car and go on to a ball game so I could be there for Jake. My support was important to him too, and it wasn't right to give myself completely to one child and not the other.

Invariably, as soon as we got settled at our stadium seats Kevin began screaming. I was never able to stay, as much as I wanted to be there for Jake. Parents and grandparents came to see their kids play ball, not to be annoyed by a screaming child.

I thought I would be less of a woman if I asked for help and I hated to whine, but the day came when that kind of thinking no longer made any sense. One night when James came home from the office, I said, "James, I can't do this by myself anymore. Please get me some help."

He looked at me like I had grits for brains.

"Aynnie, why didn't you say something before now? I've been so worried about you. My God. You look like road kill. I've been afraid to even suggest getting you some help for fear you would feel insulted or something."

"Insulted? Me? You have got to be kidding,"

He shook his head. "Of course we'll find you some help. I promise."

Later that day I cried into my bridal handkerchief until it was soaked.

Help arrived three days later when Lavonia Williams rang my doorbell. I opened the front door, saw her beautiful face and immediately burst into tears. Lavonia's mother, Pearl, had worked for my mother's family for twenty-five years. Pearl was there when Laynnie and I were born and she practically raised us. She was there when Laynnie was kidnapped and when I got married. From time to time, Pearl would bring Lavonia to work with her if extra things needed to be done, like ironing or vegetables to put up. When Lavonia got to be a teenager, Momma often called on her to babysit me. Laynnie was gone by then, of course.

Pearl died several years after I married James and because we led such different lives, I lost touch with her daughter. Lavonia was the last person on the planet I expected to see when I opened the door that day. One glance at me holding a flailing, screaming Kevin was all that was needed for Lavonia to grasp the gravity of our situation.

She stepped inside the house and said, "Aynnie, two nights ago while I was saying my prayers, I heard that baby just a-crying. It was clear as a bell. Right then I quit asking God how come bad luck always follows me around, and asked him instead how come I was hearing that baby. He said, 'Aynnie needs you.' I decided that very night that my place was here with you and those babies. That's how come I'm here."

As it turned out, Lavonia was in need of help herself. Her husband had run off with every dime they had and she lost her job as an LPN because before he left that trifling man beat her up and broke her leg. She hadn't been able to pay her rent in months and was about to be evicted.

That very day Lavonia moved into our home, and that very night I slept for the first time in Lord knows when.

When James came home that evening he was astonished to find Lavonia in the kitchen putting supper on the table like she'd been doing it all her life. He had been negotiating that same day with a domestic company and they had recommended a woman to him who he had interviewed for the housekeeping job. He had planned to talk with me about her that night.

"No need, James," I told him. By that time I had stopped bawling and was grinning like a chessie cat. "Lavonia is here and as God is my witness, she'll be here till I am so old I have to sip lamb chops through a straw. She is a miracle sent straight from God."

And she was. Within a week, Lavonia had found a way (although I never knew how) to get Kevin to stop crying and screaming. Dr. Johnson would have said Kevin's colic had run its course, but he could not have been more wrong. It was Lavonia's magic touch.

And once again, it was Lavonia who sat me down some months later and said, "Aynnie, you need to take yo' child to Duke University Hospital over in Durham. Something's going on with him that don't seem right to me."

It was Lavonia who had enough sense to put into words the fear I had carried around with me from the first moment I suckled that child and held him in my arms.

Cassie

I leaned back against the wall behind me and thought about this younger brother of Jake's. I pictured my husband, then a little boy himself, loving up on the baby and taking responsibility for his laughter and probably even some of his tears.

I also thought of Jake as a grown man. I remembered the posturing he did each time we talked about sharing our life with children of our own. He always said we would have kids later on or not at all. Now for the first time, all that kind of talk made sense to me. Jake was either afraid of passing along some kind of gene, or he was afraid of loving a child and then bearing the pain of losing it.

I knew there was more to be learned or as both Aynnie and Paul Harvey were apt to say—there was the rest of the story to be told and I wanted to hear it.

CHAPTER 21

Dear Jake's Bride,

This is a photo of dear Lavonia and it looks just like her. She was ageless thirty years ago and she still is. I told her if she could bottle her secret to staying young and beautiful she would be a millionaire. Actually, it is as much her inner beauty as anything else that even today keeps her looking like the young woman who showed up at my door that long ago day.

It was Lavonia who gave me the courage to look directly at what I had been pretending wasn't there. After our talk, I made an appointment with a noted pediatrician at Duke University Hospital and a few days later James drove us to Durham. Lavonia remained at home to take care of Jake, which was a real blessing. I didn't have one single worry about him while we were gone.

After a three-day examination by the notable neurologist, Dr. Smithline, we were invited into his office for a chat, as he called it. Once seated and we had discussed the nice weather we were having, he came to the point. I must say here that he was so very kind to us and I will be forever grateful. Within five minutes, he gave us Kevin's diagnosis and prognosis and neither one was what we wanted to hear. His words imprinted themselves on my brain where they remain to this day.

"I wish I could give you encouraging news about your boy, but unfortunately I am unable to do that. Kevin came into the world with a complex brain disorder. In laymen's language, your child was not born with the ability to process information in the same way that you and I do. Physically, he is just fine although his spatial skills will always give him a fit. Kevin will be mentally challenged but with proper guidance he can learn to function effectively. He can learn how to manage in the world even though he is different from most people."

James, looking shell-shocked and devastated, said, "What can we do? How can we help our child? There must be something."

"I'm so sorry. I wish I could tell you that things will improve as he gets older, but that will not be the case. The brain scans performed on him indicate that he will continue to have difficulty communicating and that will cause him a great deal of frustration as he gets older. He will know what he wants to say but it will be impossible to relate it to others. Using his motor skills will always be a challenge and like his social interactions will be limited. I wish I could give you more information and more hope. There is still so much we do not know about it but the upside is that we are learning more about brain function every day."

James kept shaking his head as if in denial. "But how can we help him? Is there nothing we can do? Surgery, special schools? There must be something."

The doctor, in his kindest voice said, "Love him. You can show him all the love you have to give and that will make him very happy on some level even if you are unable to see that level. You will need patience with him and it's going to be hard. When you get aggravated, try to imagine the frustration Kevin experiences every minute of every day. As hard as he will try, most of the time he will still be unable to communicate effectively with his family."

I wanted to know what we might expect with regard to his mental age and I was told that because of the many facets of brain dysfunction it was impossible to pinpoint. The doctor suggested we take it day by day and see how it goes.

At that moment, I thought I would die of heartbreak. It was as if all my inner connections, organs, blood flow, my entire being stopped working. Except for the tears.

I buried my face in the wedding handkerchief because the tears would not stop. I wanted them to, but I had lost the ability to make them obey. I wanted to scream but I didn't know how to do that. I wanted to jump out the window but my legs would not respond. I wanted to tell the doctor he was a quack and I was Kevin's mother and I was absolutely certain he would be all right in time because Dr. Johnson was *not* a quack and he said Kevin would be all right.

As devastated as James was, he picked up on my anguish and reached out to comfort me, but I shook him off. I don't know why I did that. I suppose in that moment, I didn't want to be reminded that I was wide-awake, that this was not a nightmare. I didn't want James to touch me maybe because it would make him and the entire situation all too real and I didn't want a damn thing to do with reality.

Thankfully, Dr. Smithline wrote out a tranquillizer prescription for Kevin and that made our trip back to Bear River Falls relatively peaceful. It would have been such a good thing except for the relentless tears I shed while holding the sleeping boy in my arms, too unwilling to let go of him even for a minute. Kevin hung onto Boo Bear as though it were a lifeline to normalcy. Seeing him like that, make me cry harder.

Life goes on, even when you are convinced that it must be close to an end. It continues although you feel certain you cannot live through one more day with your heart breaking piece-by-piece and minute-by-minute. But somehow you do.

It was a struggle. Eventually we reached the point where we could accept and absorb all that we learned at Duke regarding Kevin's condition. Only when we allowed the information to infiltrate our daily lives were did we become capable of carrying on. Carrying on is what we did, and we did it as well as anyone could have.

As Kevin got older, instead of his behavior improving during mealtime, our family suppers in particular turned into mayhem. Even though Lavonia was willing to feed the boy separately, I insisted that Kevin remained at the table with the rest of the family unless he was physically ill. I was determined that he should be included as much as possible in whatever the rest of us were doing, but that inclusion made life incredibly difficult for all of us.

It was not an unusual occurrence for Kevin to pick up a chicken drumstick and, grinning all the while, toss it across the table for Jake to catch. Jake was a good little athlete so he always managed to catch it. He would then patiently, with a smile on his face, take it over to Kevin and put it back on his plate where it belonged.

"Don't throw the drumstick, Kev," he would say gently. "Eat it like this!" Jake would pick up another chicken leg and bite into it in order to show him how it was supposed to be done. Kevin would then grin at his brother and take a bite of his own chicken leg but before Jake even returned to his chair, the drumstick was airborne again.

Table conversation was impossible. As if finally discovering that he liked the sound of his voice, Kevin was louder than any of the rest of us and he constantly interrupted. Sometimes Jake was able to get him to lower his voice a little, but within minutes, Kevin would laugh and begin talking and shouting all over again.

Lavonia, on the other hand, could whisper something in Kevin's ear and the boy was immediately calm and he would remain that way for the rest of the meal. I have no idea what it was she said to him, and she never divulged her secret.

Between Jake and Lavonia, Kevin was the recipient of two of the best friends a person could ever hope to know. I thanked God for them both, not just when I prayed at night, but throughout the day I found myself blessing them both.

Cassie

I so want to command the clock to stop ticking for the rest of the day so that I can go through the entire trunk like Sherman through Atlanta. I ache to read every word and every thought that went into the letters written by this woman who had given birth to my husband and his baby brother. I wanted to immerse myself in her days, her pain, and her joys.

But—life has a nasty habit of producing too many buts, doesn't it? When I look up from the belly of the trunk and gaze through the attic window at the setting sun, it becomes clear to me that it is time to halt my secret life for another day. I need to resume that other life with all of its buts, the one made up of cooking, cleaning and morphing into the wife Jake McMinns thought he knew, the one he greeted at the end of each day.

If I didn't figure out how to balance my two lives, I was going to need a shrink or a drink. Maybe both.

CHAPTER 22

Dear Jake's Bride,

For many years, we owned a cottage in Georgia on St. Simons Island and that is where we vacationed for a month each summer. It was always a big deal for us to go down there because everything about it was so different from Western North Carolina.

The boys loved it so. When Kevin was old enough, Jake took him crabbing. It was something they both could do because Jake was right there to help Kevin if and when his line got tangled or if they were lucky enough to catch any crabs.

They didn't go swimming because Kevin didn't know how, but they walked for endless miles along the beach collecting shells and sharks teeth if they could find them. I had a tough time getting them to come in from the beach. They loved being out there. By the time we came back to North Carolina both of them had been toasted by the sun and looked healthier than ever.

One year, Jake took Kevin out for a walk, ostensibly looking for more petrified shark's teeth to add to Kevin's growing collection. As soon as they were away from the house (and me), Kevin started bugging his brother to let him wade at the water's edge. Knowing that if he gave Kevin an inch the boy would try to take a mile, so he said no.

"You don't know how to swim, Kev, and you might trip and fall in. The undertow is real strong today. It's way too dangerous for you or anybody. Do you understand that word? Dangerous?"

Kevin frowned. "Don't care," he said. "I want to go in the water and swim."

Jake said, "Not today, Kev. Maybe I'll take you in the water tomorrow."

They walked on for a bit picking up shells, looking all over the place for shark's teeth or an occasional piece of wampum, shells with splashes of the color purple the Indians used for money back in the day.

Jake instructed Kevin to wait for him by the jetty while he went to pick up a box he had spied on a dune. "We need something to put our shells in," he explained. "Now, wait right here for me and don't you move. I'll be right back."

Just as Jake reached the top of the dune Kevin spied a sea gull skimming across the water's edge. That was all it took. He dropped the shells he had collected and ran like the wind after the gull.

When Jake looked up and saw what was happening, he yelled and took off after his little brother but it was high tide, the wind was up and waves were loudly crashing. There was no way Kevin could have heard his brother yelling for him to stop. In no time at all, Kevin was in the water up to his knees and he kept on going as though he was running on sand.

It was early morning and rather cool for a Georgia summer, so both boys were wearing long jeans that day. Even so, Jake plunged into the water after his brother, heavy clothes and all. Kevin, as though guided by an invisible force had a head start so he kept moving out, heedless of his brother's pleas for him to stop and come back to shore.

Jake, fighting the incoming tide and strong undertow, stumbled and then got up only to stumble into the water again. Kevin would stumble too, but each time he got up and continued chasing the sea gull, oblivious to Jake's pleas.

Jake saw Kevin stumble again but that time he went under, head and all and did not come back up. He struggled to reach him but was pushed back by the incoming waves fighting him like a mighty wind. When he was finally within reach and could have grabbed Kevin's body out of the water, his brother had completely disappeared. He was gone.

Had Jake been able to reach him in time, they both might have drowned. Jake would have had to fight the undertow while trying to hold his brother's head up out of the water. In fact, Jake was pulled under water several times. Fortunately, a man walking along the beach saw what was happening, and without another thought, rushed into the water to save him.

Jake fought the man hard while screaming out his brother's name, but the man was a stranger and didn't understand that there was another boy in trouble. When they finally reached the shore, even though Jake was hysterical, he was able to get through to the man and make him understand that his brother was still in the water. By that time, however, Kevin had been swept out to sea. His little body washed up on shore two days later.

Jake never forgave himself for this tragedy. He always blamed himself for his brother's drowning. In my opinion, this is one of the reasons, if not the primary reason, he refuses to go back up to the attic.

I'm sure you have noticed how we turned the entire area into a growing boy's private playground, complete with a basketball goal, shuffleboard, playing cards and such. It was a great place for them both when the weather was bad and they couldn't go out to play. I can't begin to count the hours those two spent upstairs, but even today I can still hear the thump, thump, thump of a basketball.

After the accident, we sold the St. Simons beach house. None of us could delete from our lives the memory of that awful tragedy. Had we kept the house, it would have been a sad Kevin connection that none of us would have been able to bear.

Years passed but still Jake never stopped feeling responsible for Kevin's death. He was able to tell us in detail exactly how the accident occurred but after that he refused to even mention his little brother's name. To my knowledge he has never gone back up to the attic.

This is enough for today.

I remain your loving mother-in-law, Aynnie

Cassie

Oh my God. I feel as though I have been showered in too much family history, drenched. I am not sure I can take it all in. When I think of what Jake has been going through alone for so many years, my heart splinters. If only he had trusted me enough to confide in me. Could I have eliminated his feelings of guilt? Of course not. Could I have smoothed salve on his emotional bruises? Of course I could have. Why didn't he let me in?

I go downstairs to think, think, think. Later when I feel collected enough to make even a lick of sense I pull my thoughts together and take a deep breath. That's when I make the decision to go ahead and do what I should have done weeks ago.

It is Friday, the one night of the week when Jake and I have our standard date night. After enjoying a nice dinner and a beautiful bottle of wine at a mountaintop restaurant overlooking the lush meadow below, we drive for a little while along the Blue Ridge Parkway. Jake's week has been another stressful one so a quiet drive seems to be just the thing to help pull him back into a better place.

"Jake, I want you to tell me about your brother Kevin, and then I want to know more about your dad. You hardly ever talk about him and I've inundated you with facts about mine."

My husband momentarily looks away from the road. His face is one of complete surprise; his brows are hooked together to form a big "V" in the center of his forehead.

"What did you say?"

I know he's stalling for time but the moment, as they say on the Cialis commercials, seems right and I don't know if or when the moment will seem right again. I smile at my husband the lawyer who thinks I don't know that his thoughts are whirling around in his head like a broken helicopter.

"Kevin," I say. "I want to know all about your little brother, Jake."

"There's nothing to tell, Cassie." Jake's voice is beyond cool. "I had a brother. He died. End of story."

I don't say anything right away. I hope by keeping quiet my husband will intuit that I am still waiting for him to open up and talk to me. After a few minutes, he does.

"Cassie, who told you about Kevin?"

Talk about a loaded question I was not prepared to answer. However, I figure it's as good a time as any to dump my secret on him. If our marriage is not strong enough for either of us to be open with each other, even when it's painful, then I need to know now rather than later. It is up to me to begin.

"Jake, I went up to the attic not too long ago. You remember we talked about it a while back and you said you had no interest in going up there with me. Well, I was bored one day and decided to go on up there and explore. Wow. You never told me there was an entire game parlor in the attic."

"Yeah, well ..."

I take a deep breath. "Once I got up there I wanted to see everything. Jake, I had expected it to be a big pile of discarded junk but it's not like that at all. A person could live up there."

He sighs and I notice that it is not a sigh of relief but rather one that has lived in his lungs for far too long. "A while back," he says, "somebody almost did. So did you see a picture of Kevin, while you were roaming around up there or what? Like I told you before, I haven't been to the attic in years."

And now I know why, I think. "A picture? You could say that. I saw one of the two of you, but you were both very young. Jake, I really want you to talk to me about this and help me to understand why you never told me you had a brother. Gosh darn it, you know everything there is to know about me and a lot I'd as soon you didn't. I feel like you only let me see a piece of you and Jake, darling, I want to see all of you. The good, bad and indifferent. Warts and all."

He pulls the car over and parks at an overlook with a magnificent mountain view. We silent for a minute or two before he suggests we get out and sit on one of the benches nicely provided by the state of North Carolina Parks Service.

"Cassie, I don't talk about Kevin because it was a long time ago and he died and there was an accident and I guess I just never really got over it."

I reach over and take his hand. "It might be good for you to talk about it, Jake, even though it is painful. Can you tell me a little about Kevin before the accident?"

Again, the deep, long sigh.

"You may have noticed in the picture that we looked a lot alike. Brothers do, I'm told. We were born almost four years apart and I remember the day Momma and Daddy brought him home from the hospital. I fell in love with him on sight, pretty much like I did when I saw you. He was such a beautiful baby and, knowing that he was my brother, I couldn't stop grinning. I was staring at him in the little cradle when I asked Momma if we could keep him."

Remembering that day, Jake actually smiles.

"What did she say to that?" I am smiling too.

He laughs. "She said, 'Keep him? Jake, he's not a stray puppy who just wandered up to the kitchen door. Of course we can keep him. He's one of us now and he always will be.' I reached down and felt his little face and when I did it made me so happy."

I squeeze my husband's hand and then tucked my head on his shoulder.

"Turned out, Cassie, Kevin was not like other children. He was what today is called a special needs kid. That's the politically correct term we are supposed to use."

I nod. I really want him to continue talking even though I have already been told the entire story. I am hoping Jake will tell me in his own words because at some point, maybe not tonight, I plan to fess up, too. I will tell him all about the trunk and everything I have learned from his mother's letters. I don't want to reveal anything tonight because something tells me that there is more I need to see in the attic before I spill my guts. More pictures, more letters from Aynnie. More family history.

"After we found out why he struggled so hard to communicate with us, I sort of took him on as my pet project, so to speak. We were very close, Kev and me. I was able to tell what he wanted or needed at those times when he was unable to communicate with anybody else. And he trusted me, dammit."

Those five words seemed to turn into a dagger. "He trusted me and I let him down."

I wait, not daring to make any comment while I hope Jake will continue talking. After a minute or so when he doesn't say anything more, I ask how he had let his brother down.

I have only seen Jake with tears in his eyes one other time. He cried when I told him that my parents were victims of the 9-11 Trade Center tragedy. Now I watch my husband's eyes fill with tears hoping that the button I just pushed will take Jake to a better emotional place if only he will allow it.

"Kevin drowned and it was all my fault. I should have ..." He covers his face in his hands and sobs. It breaks my heart to see him like this.

After a bit, he straightens up and tells me his own memory of the accident using almost the identical words that Aynnie had written. When he stops talking, he sits very still and stares out at the vast forests below.

"Jake, preventing your brother's accident was impossible. Think about it. You were just a kid yourself. I've read enough about children with special needs to know that once their focus is set on something, everything else flies out of the window."

Jake looks at me as though I can't possibly understand his pain and then he looks away. Shaking his head he says, "Don't patronize me, Cassie.

"I'm not doing that, Jake. I love you and I'm so sorry this awful thing happened. I'm sorry about Kevin and the struggles he endured during his life. But I'm also sad that you never confided to me how you have been feeling all these years. It explains a lot of things I didn't understand. You need to let it go, darling. Kevin would want you to do that. It's time."

He sighs again, one of those golly whopper sighs. "Yeah, you're right, but it's a lot harder than you might think."

I stand up, still holding his hand. "I want us to continue this talk again some time soon and I need you to tell me all about the rest of your family because they are my family too. But for now, let's go home."

And we do.

CHAPTER 23

Dear Jake's Bride,

Kevin's death hurled us all into an emotional abyss so deep it seemed we would not, could not survive. Jake harbored enormous feelings of guilt and he was not the only one. What was I doing while my two sons fought the undertow in the Atlanta Ocean, while my oldest son struggled with all his might to save his little brother, while my little boy, my helpless baby was drowning? I was in the house writing a letter to my friend back in Bear River Falls telling her the difficulties of coping with a special needs child.

Because Jake was Kevin's self-proclaimed protector since the infant child came home from the hospital, I'd had no qualms about allowing the two of them to roam the beach together. Jake was a responsible boy and I felt he would, as he always did, take care of Kevin. It never crossed my mind, not even once, that something so tragic could or would happen to them. Never!

I knew how impetuous Kevin was, but we had come so far in learning how to deal more effectively with his impulsivity. We overcame a great deal while blending as a family.

There was no way to predict what happened so maybe it was supposed to be. For my own sanity, I have tried to talk myself into believing that it was God's will. Predestination. Fate. Whatever name came to mind. That kind of thinking helped me to keep the faith when I so needed to believe that nothing could have prevented Kevin's death.

For years, I tried to talk to Jake along these lines. I talked until my face turned the color of a blueberry, but he locked that door the day his brother died and he was bound and determined to leave it that way. I tried to understand and there were times when I did. It was a lot for a twelve-year-old boy to deal with and the bottom line is that he did what he had to do.

That said, as Jake's mother and as one who has also lived with the devastating loss of a sibling, it is my strong belief that he must one day unlock and open that closed door if he is to go forward. Until he clears away all of the baggage he's collected over the years, he won't be able to love a child again without the fear of something awful happening to that child.

As I mentioned, Jake was not the only one horribly affected by Kevin's death. James convinced himself that he had not been a good enough father to the boy, and he may have been right about that. At least partially right. I think Kevin frightened James. He never knew quite how to be present with a child born with complicated communication issues. In James's defense, he missed out on the day-to-day hands-on interaction that Lavonia, Jake and I had with Kevin. We learned the nuances because we were there and because we had to. What James had to do was go to work.

Even so, he felt guilty for not giving more of himself to the boy and guilt is a high price to pay. Too high. When James's health began to decline, he ignored all of the warning signs. About that same time, I saw him taking a lot of unnecessary risks.

I begged him to see a doctor when his weight dropped noticeably but he refused. He worked longer hours at the office and, although he had never been a teetotaler, his one or two glasses of wine turned into whatever it took to get him drunk enough to stop blaming himself for not being a better father and husband.

Our relationship suffered drastically. At a time when we needed to be there for each other, we were light years apart. On the other hand, he doted on Jake to the point of obsession. His behavior reminded me so much of how my father responded after Laynnie was taken.

Jake got involved in school activities and that is where he dumped all of his grief stricken energies. I suspect he did so on purpose but I was not so fortunate.

Lavonia left us after a few months and to me it was like a second death. Her husband, the sorry dog, came back to her with promises of good behavior and God knows what all, so she chose to believe him. With Kevin gone, Jake immersed in school and James in his work, Lavonia felt she was no longer needed. I would have given anything for her to stay because I was bereft and more needy than I ever admitted to anyone, but Lavonia deserved better. I knew that. I'm not saying she deserved that husband of hers, but if there was a shred of hope for their marriage, then she had no choice but to take him back and try again.

In time, I found myself wandering up those 14 steps to the attic where I often sat picturing my two boys playing together in the outer room. There were days when I thought I could actually hear them laughing and teasing one another and I would cry. My wedding handkerchief got so wet with tears I could have wrung it out like a washcloth.

The small room was the only place in the house where I felt safe enough to let go and cry my heart out. The tears I shed were not just for the loss of Kevin but also for my sister Laynnie. I was never able to shed enough tears for her. That remains the case even today.

What became an attic bedroom was originally a storage area. A junk room, really. But with my marriage disassembling almost daily, and with nothing much to anchor me to the downstairs part of the house, I decided to turn the storage room into something more practical—a space just for me.

At first I only used it during the day. I would sit in the wing chair and read until I got sleepy and often I would lie down on the bed and take a nap. That pattern went on for a few months. I only came downstairs when I heard Jake come home from school or from football practice. Eventually, he got more and more involved in after-school activities and wouldn't come home until dark. By that time he had perfected his ability to avoid me completely. He would fix himself a sandwich and then go straight up to his room to study where he remained until the next morning when it was time for him to leave the house again.

James came home later and later and hardly ever wanted anything to eat, so it was a simple thing for me to stay put in my self-designed sanctuary. When eventually I began to spend my nights there as well, I doubt James even noticed.

Our family continued to splinter and none of us knew what to do about it or even if we wanted to do anything. It would take yet another tragedy for things to turn around but even then, the fragile relationship between Jake and me remained on shaky ground.

I can't say that James's death, as horrible as it was, came as too much of a surprise. It was tragic and sad and senseless, but on some level I was aware that he no longer wanted to live with himself. I knew how he felt because I didn't want to be ME anymore either.

He didn't need to take a gun out to the woods and blow his brains out for me to understand what he was going through, but that is exactly what he did.

Once again I have become maudlin in the recounting of those heartbreaking days and I hope you will forgive me. I want these accounts of my life to be honest because for so long I kept all of my feelings a big secret, much like my Jake did and probably still does.

At the same time, I want you to keep in mind that we survived the hardest possible struggles a family can experience and that is a good thing. It is a very good thing.

It was not easy, but in time Jake and I managed to come out of the gloom of death that haunted us after the loss of husband, father, son and brother. We journeyed the road to recovery, albeit on separate paths but we were able to find daylight out of darkness and gloom and I am so very proud of us for that.

With love from Aynnie

Cassie

I feel torn up inside! Given all of the times since I've known Jake McMinns, plus all the many hours I have talked at length about the tragic death of *my* parents, he never, never, never mentioned that his father had committed suicide.

I don't know whether to be totally pissed at him or what. Obviously that is not a subject a son wants to broadcast to the world, but good God Almighty! I am his wife, his best friend. I deserve better.

CHAPTER 24

Dear Jake's Bride,

You must be puzzled by this stack of old credit card receipts and check stubs among my photos and memorabilia. You must be wondering what possible significance they could hold for the McMinns. As you will see, there are a number of them and you will also notice that a woman's signature appears on quite a few of them. Although James signed them most of the time, you won't find Aynnie McMinns's signature no matter how hard you look.

I want you to see them all. No need to make a study of them—just leaf through them so you can get an idea of the sheer number, and for how long a time they continued.

Tommie Sue Taggert was bound and determined to reenter and become a part our lives, and I suppose deep down I always knew it would happen sooner or later. But like with so many other issues in my life, I didn't want to acknowledge it. She played a large role in James's life but I didn't have enough sense to pay attention to what was happening right in front of me.

Why do you suppose that was? I think it was because my son died and for a long, long time I too, was drowning too, just not at the beach in St. Simons Island. I was drowning in grief.

The packed dirt on James's grave barely had time to level out when I received a phone call from Bruce Hunt, James's closest friend and partner in the law firm of McMinns, Hunt and Stevens.

"Hey, Aynnie," he began. "How are things going with you?"

I stopped myself from blurting out, "My husband committed suicide and before that, my youngest son drowned. My other son and I both feel responsible and are drowning in guilt, so at the moment the two of us are emotionally incapable of carrying on a simple conversation with each other. Consequently, I feel I am losing him, too. Just how the hell do you suppose things are going with me, Bruce?"

But I didn't say all that. I only thought it.

"We're very sad, Bruce. It's been such a hard thing to deal with, but we're trying. Thank you for asking."

That's what I said.

He cleared his throat and asked if he might come over that same afternoon to discuss some details regarding James's Will.

Alarm bells went off in my head but even then I didn't have sense enough to figure out why that was. Having been a lawyer's daughter before becoming married to one, I lived with most of the ins and outs of civil law all of my life. James and I made out a Will together and the firm put the finishing touches on it. As far as I knew, no details needed to be discussed.

"Bruce," I said to him, "can it wait? Surely, the firm can handle whatever it is until I am in a better place. I'm very familiar with the Will that you drew up for us, and to my recollection it's cut and dried. Unless something has come up recently that I know nothing about, then I beg you to please take care of it for me. Can you do that?"

I cannot describe the depth of trepidation I felt in that moment. I am certain you have heard the old expression "waiting for the other shoe to drop." Well, that was the feeling I had while on the phone with Bruce Hunt that day, only it felt more like waiting for a refrigerator to drop down on top of me.

Listen to me now because I am about to impart some wise advice: always, always trust your woman's intuition.

Bruce cleared his throat again. "There are just a few things I think we should go over together, Aynnie, and it shouldn't take long. I realize the timing is inconvenient and that you'd rather wait till later, but we need to take care of it this afternoon."

I sighed and told him to come around after lunch and he thanked me and hung up. I was left to ask myself why such intense feelings of dread were rocking my soul from the bottom up. What I should have asked myself was, 'What are you pretending not to know this time, Aynnie?'

When Bruce arrived at two o'clock that afternoon, one look at his face and I knew I was about to be assaulted with information I did not want to hear. The expression on his face was the same as the one he wore while delivering James's eulogy, and for just a moment I thought he had come to deliver the news that someone else I cared about had died.

I invited him inside and we sat in the living room.

"Can I get you something," I asked, hoping for a small reprieve. "Iced tea? Coke? Something stronger?"

He thanked me and said he had just eaten a huge dinner at the Club. "Marian has threatened to leave me if I don't quit eating such heavy meals in the middle of the day. But I do so love to eat and the food at the Club is so good that I can't resist it."

I was already tired of the chitchat. "So, what's this all about, Bruce?"

His briefcase was open and he was pulling out a stack of papers, including the receipts I later put in the trunk for you to find. He sighed as though he would rather be chewing up a piece of granite than having to have this conversation with me. That made two of us.

"Aynnie, do you know a woman by the name of Tommie Sue Taggert?"

With that one question, I was able to figure out the reason for his visit.

As it turned out, my husband had been carrying on with his former fiancée for years. I didn't ask Bruce how long the affair had been going on, but I suspect it started when the boys were very young, probably soon after she made that phone call to him at our home.

Not long after James died and while Jake and I were in the midst of using every cell in our bodies and souls to deal with his suicide and all of its ramifications, Tommie Sue Taggert decided to contest James's Last Will and Testament. She claimed that my husband had promised to leave a lump what Bruce had come to my house to discuss with me.

To begin with, we didn't have that much money and the law firm had no intention of ponying it up, nor should they have. I told Bruce to take her ass to court because in lawyer speak, the whole damn thing was moot. Even so, it made me mad as hell that a grubby piece of trash like her dared to interrupt my family's grieving process in order to line her pockets.

Thinking of my husband in bed with another woman for so many of the years I had thought we were living happily ever after was so very painful. All couples go through bad times but having that woman try to wash our dirty laundry in the very courts to which James had devoted his life was simply unacceptable.

It was hard on Jake, too, who was already wading through knee-deep anger at his father for having killed himself. That was hard enough on the boy, but then to have to deal with the news that his father had cheated on his wife and family, well, it was too much. I feel certain the damage done to my son during that time can never be completely undone.

As it turned out, Bruce Hunt told Tommie Sue that the amount of money she demanded was unavailable in James's estate and that the firm held an ironclad Will that did not include any allowance for her. When she was told that little bit of news, she tucked her switching little tail and backed off. We never heard from her again but like I said, the damage was done. There is no way to unring a bell.

I am reminded of a quote by the actor Nishan Panwar. I read it while trying to deal with my husband's betrayal. "Be careful home wreckers. Go ahead and mess with someone else's man knowingly. One day your most treasured relationship will be ruined in the same way. Karma!"

In recounting this ugly ordeal on paper, I realize how angry I still am at James as well as that home wrecker bitch Tommie Sue. Because of my seething anger and also because she and James are both history now—

water under the bridge—I won't write about or speak of it again.

I have no excess energy these days because there is only a little left to me. I refuse to squander it because my old body just might not tolerate any more negativity.

My days are winding down more quickly than I want them to, so I am choosing not to dwell on the bad things in my past that I had no control over back then. Even if I'd had any control, it is not often that life offers do-overs.

Love from Aynnie

Cassie

Holding the letter in one hand, I snatch up the cluster of receipts with the other. It is a very large stack. I am no longer curious as to why Aynnie included something I had at first thought was so banal. After reading her letter and now as I look at each one of the receipts as well as a faded matchbook, I easily grasp the substance of James's expenditures. I have no need to wonder what they were all about. James was keeping a mistress; her name was Tommie Sue Taggert and he spent a bunch of money on her. The only thing I wonder about now is whether or not he actually included this woman in his final Will. I sincerely hope not. That would have been an even harder pill for Aynnie to swallow.

My God. The secrets in this family are piling up higher than those at the CIA. And once again, I was not given even one clue.

I realize that, unlike many women, men are seldom direct when it comes to sharing personal stuff, but I can't help being angry at Jake for not telling me these things and I can't help but feel that I don't really know the man I married. I thought I did.

Until a few minutes ago my impression of Jake's mother and father had been that they were the perfect couple with issues that were resolved over time. They managed somehow to survive. I am still reeling over the fact that Jake's father took his own life and that Jake never once mentioned it. So maybe suicide is not something one talks about easily, but I am his wife. Suicide is a big something and he should have shared it with me no matter how much it hurt.

The fact that I am in the process of discovering family secrets in a secretive way myself suddenly punches me in the gut. Hard. How can I judge Jake when I am basically doing the same thing? Is there something intrinsic in the McMinns family tree that dictates we should hide things from each other?

Questions. So many questions. So many unanswered questions.

I am thinking about another of Aynnie's letters, the one in which she wrote about the day Tommie Sue called her on the phone asking for James. The call had come at the end of a hectic day when the boys were still young, almost babies. Surely, James was not carrying on with this Tommie Sue Taggert at that time and even all the years afterward.

As my best friend and step-sister Jillie might say, "Oy vey! What next?"

I look at my watch and realize that once again, my other life is feeling neglected and, as it happens so often these days, I seem to have lost all track of time. I need to buy groceries if we are to ever sit down at our own table for a meal again. I also need to take Miss Priss to the vet to have her nails clipped before she fatally wounds me. I need to pick up a reserved library book written on the history of the Great Depression. Jennifer, the librarian I've come to know and love called this morning to let me know she's holding it for me.

You ask what next, Jillie? The Attic Saga will just have to wait.

CHAPTER 25

Dear Jake's Wife,

Last night I had a strange dream that won't let go of me, and given my current physical state I figure it is significant. As bizarre as it may seem, I may have been sent a memo, a more urgent one than when my doctor told me to get my affairs in order. I feel the need to share the dream with someone but who would that be? I don't want to have a conversation with Jake about this because he wouldn't get it. In addition, I'm sure it would upset him to think that my days are numbered even though surely he must already be aware of it. Jake, my good boy, does not want to think about dark tomorrows.

In this case, I believe the safest thing to do is to write my dream to you, Jake's wife. It will do me good to get it out of my system and by the time you read it, my projection of it being prophetic will be a moot point anyway. So here goes.

I was traveling in no particular hurry through the neighborhoods of my youth. I was driving a small German car I named Axis Sally after the World War II German propagandist. Sally seemed to have a mind of her own when she nosed into my old friend Ann's circular driveway. Ann and I were in school together but I've not seen her in over fifty years. Nevertheless, in my dream I had no trouble finding her grey brick house with the rust colored shutters and white trim around the windows. Sally applied the brakes dead center by Ann's front door and I craned my neck hoping to glimpse my old friend. When no one appeared, Axis Sally revved the motor and took off.

I told myself I needed to get on home because I had supper to cook. My family would be hungry when they came in.

Without giving a turn signal, Axis Sally swerved to the right and onto a street as familiar to me as my own face. We drove in no particular hurry but with a mutual destination in mind: home. To my left was a house I recognized; across the street on the right was the Smith's home.

Sally kept going while I looked all around in search of my own house.

"There it is on the left. That's it," I said aloud and breathed easier as relief infused my mind and body. My headstrong car turned into the driveway but at the last moment I realized it was not my house after all. It was where the Henderson's lived.

"Keep on trucking, Sal," I told the car as if it had ears and could actually hear me. "Turn right on Fourth Street," I added.

We coasted downhill while I looked from one window to the next, trying in vain to find where I lived. Instead of home, however, we were suddenly in the middle of a construction area where houses were being built, roads reconstructed. It was foreign while yet familiar.

I was lost, lost inside the streets of my past and I can't tell you how alone and frightened I felt. By then, even Axis Sally had abandoned me. I set out on foot toward a construction worker busy repairing a dilapidated house.

"I'm sorry to bother you," I said to him, "but I think I may be lost."

The man appeared to be in charge. He smiled and tipped his hard hat away from his face; he looked like the Marlboro Man.

"Where do you want to go," he asked.

"Home," I said. "I need to go home."

He raised his eyebrows. "And that would be *where*?"

I realized then that I didn't know where my home was anymore. I thought I did, but when I pictured the house in my mind's eye, the image immediately changed to the house we lived in when James and I were first married, but that was no longer my home.

I told the man, "It's the house with swings in the side yard and two little boys chasing each other. There will be a dog barking at them both. The house has dark green shutters..."

He shook his head, shrugged his shoulders. "Sorry, lady. Can't help you."

I felt numb but I climbed the steps to the dilapidated house with its screen door ajar. Inside, I walked down a hall crammed with pieces of furniture that looked vaguely familiar. I think perhaps they had once belonged to James and me. There was a slightly marred dresser, the one we bought at auction when we were newlyweds. A heavier chest was shoved behind it, its drawers askew.

I looked up and saw three closed doors leading to three separate rooms. Stepping around the pieces of furniture (that were once mine), I headed for the last door, the one at the far end of the hall. My hand closed around the knob and it turned. The door opened.

I gasped.

There was one single bed in the room over which was spread a worn blue coverlet. There was one pillow; there was no headboard. Two undressed windows looked back at me as though embarrassed for not wearing curtains. The walls might have been white at one time but framed pictures no long hung on it, only old nails where pictures had once lived.

As I looked at the naked walls, a profound sadness washed over me and before I knew it, a storm of tears was crashing like a tsunami down my face.

Standing very still in the doorway, I gazed into a room that my mind told me had once been occupied by a child, although no children had been inside of it for a long time. I don't know how I knew this, but I did. It was a make-do bedroom, completely devoid of personality.

There were no flowers, mirrors or books, no chipped figurines or drooping candles. The old nails stuck in the faded walls were the only reminder of what used to be. It was the saddest room I had ever seen, and I wept for the solitude I sensed inside of it.

When I awoke, without having to think about it, I knew who had once lived in that room. I knew who had hung pictures on the walls and who had kept a child's keepsakes on the bare table next to the bed. It was my Kevin's old room, but the emptiness belonged only to me.

The dream made me acutely aware that my time here will soon be up.

Cassie

I shove the cat off my lap and even manage to survive the scathing look she gives me for dumping her. Since the library is on the way to Fresh Market, I stop off to pick up the Great Depression book Jennifer is holding for me. Just after I finish writing my name on the library card for a Walker Evans book of Depression photographs, someone bumps into me. There is a loud thump and then a crash. I twirl around like Baryshnikov on speed.

An elderly man is lying on the floor looking perfectly mortified. He tries to get up but for whatever reason is unable to manage it.

I reach out. "Grab my hand and I'll pull you up."

He looks at me with warmth, his eyes clearly full of embarrassment and discomfort. He reminds me of Clarence Oddbody in *It's a Wonderful Life*, my favorite Christmas flick.

Seven or eight books are scattered all over the floor and surround him. They are books on loan that I assume he was about to return before he rear-ended me. When he is back on his feet again, I kneel down to help him gather up the errant books.

"No need to do that, my dear. I can manage now. Just tripped over myself and lost my balance, one of the many hazards of dotage, I'm afraid."

Laughing, I tell him that I do the same thing no less than twice a week and I'm not yet ready to apply for Social Security. It's a lie, but I sense that he is a gentle soul and I feel the need to say something that will make him feel less awkward about falling.

"Here you go." I hand him three of the books. Glancing down I notice the titles he is returning and it is impressive. Baruch Spinoza's Ethics, Nietzsche. I am further surprised when I see some other titles: Descartes on mind–body dualism, as well as the philosopher and historian Friedrich Hegel. Interesting selection.

"I don't believe I've had the pleasure of meeting you," I say to the old man. "Close encounters of the third kind don't really count. I'm Cassie McMinns and you are?"

His face sighs, if that is possible. "McMinns," he says. "And I will wager a guess that you are the bride of young Jake McMinns, Esquire."

Smiling broadly, I say, "Guilty as charged. How do you know Jake?"

He walks over to Jennifer's desk and plops down the heavy books. "Whew. The worst thing about philosophers is that they don't know when to shut up." He laughs. "I'm Tom Langston, Cassie. And Jake?

Well, your husband and I go way back. I taught him in school, you see, and his mother God rest her soul, was a very dear friend of mine."

"You knew Aynnie? Oh, I'm so happy we bumped into each other, Mr. Langston. It's wonderful to meet someone who was a friend of Aynnie's. She died before Jake and I met, but the more I learn about her the sadder I am that I never knew her."

He looks at me for a long moment, not a stare exactly, more like an extended thoughtful kind of look, as though reading my face or peering inside my soul.

"People around here call me Mr. Tom. Using sir names in the South is akin to wearing a tuxedo to a garage sale."

I laugh at the analogy and agree with him.

"Cassie, your mother-in-law was one of the most delightful people in Bear River Falls. When she died, she didn't leave a hole, she left a crater. Now, what do you think of that? Kind of negates all those mean, crabby mother-in-law online jokes, doesn't it?"

Almost as a mutual non-verbal agreement, the two of us amble over to a vacant table and sit down across from each other. It is still early in the morning and the library is virtually empty, so we have the freedom to talk in a normal voice without having to whisper. There are so many questions I want to ask him but I don't. No need to bombard the man when we've only just met.

He comments on my Walker Evans book and tells me that his uncle once met Mr. Evans. I was once again impressed. Then he began to talk about the McMinns.

"I've known Jake all of his life. Knew his daddy too. He was the attorney that handled all three of my divorces. Yes he did. James was a good man and was mourned by a lot of people in this town when he died."

"I've heard many kind things said about him," I say, "and it's a good feeling to know that I married into such a fine family."

There is no way in hell I will ask him about Tommie Sue Taggert. I will agree to be strung upside down on a makeshift cross before that ugly piece of gossip escapes my lips.

Mr. Tom gives me his *I'm inside your soul* look again. "I suppose you know by now, all about the tragic death of the younger boy, Jake's little brother. Kevin, I think his name was. It was a terrible thing. So sad. The long and short of it is that James never got over it. When that child died, he lapsed into a deep depression that grew and grew. I can only imagine the demons that haunted James's every waking moment."

I tell him that I know about Kevin and also how Jake's father died, but I don't reveal my source. Looking into his face, I suspect he thinks

Jake is the one who confided in me and I don't say anything to make him think otherwise.

There are a thousand questions bubbling up in my mind, but something tells me to go easy. I intuit that we will become good friends, Mr. Tom and me, and hopefully there will be more interesting conversations in our future.

After a while of getting-to-know-you-chit-chat, I tell him I have to go to the grocery store and pick up my cat from the vet. "It's been a pleasure getting to know you, Mr. Tom. If you're not afraid to eat my cooking, maybe you'll come over one night for supper? I've been told that I am actually a microwave maven."

"You are very kind, Cassie, and I would love to come to supper. It's been a good while since I've been in the McMinns house and I understand Jake remodeled it after Aynnie died. I'd be most interested to see how that turned out."

As though he is a long-lost relative, I reach over and kiss my new friend on the cheek and then follow it with a hefty hug. He grins like I just handed him a winning lottery ticket.

I so wish Aynnie and I could talk—really talk. I would tell her that I have a big crush on her old buddy and that I think she had excellent taste in friends.

That will have to wait until I'm once again sprawled out on the floor in the attic leafing through her trunk of memories.

CHAPTER 26

Dear Jake's Bride,

Normally, I find it frustrating knowing that I will have to wait for the last hard freeze of the season in Bear River Falls. I so love this area right after the cold earth has woken up and is soaring into spring with blooms that shout rebirth. It is then that I throw off my overcoat and heavy sweaters and take to wandering around in my yard.

I am no environmentalist, although I do love nature and never fail to be astonished at what it can accomplish in a relatively short time. Seems like only yesterday I huddled inside my house wrapped up in a Snuggie that my friend Becky gave me for Christmas. (Snuggies are the best invention ever devised for old brittle bones!) Almost over night some of the daffodils have popped out all over the meadow below as if they are the opening act for what will follow.

There are seven Dogwood trees in my yard and by mid-April the green buds have burst into bloom like popcorn. Those beautiful four-cornered, white flowering trees present themselves at Eastertide each year. I stand back and applaud nature, ever thankful for the Dogwood Tree. Whether intentional or not, it reminds me that life goes on. After what I have been through and knowing what lies ahead, nature's ability to keep on keeping on is a welcome piece of news.

I write this letter for two reasons. One of course is so that you will continue in your quest to know the history of the family to which you have become a member. The other reason is more personal and is directed only to you. This is the letter that will answer your questions and tell you so much more about the man we both love dearly — our Jake.

The spring following James's suicide, I needed as many reminders of life as I could find. The previous months had been cruel and I often thought of a line in Shakespeare's Richard III: "Now is the winter of our discontent..." Without a doubt, it was MY winter of discontent and the longest season I ever spent. I was cold all of the time and could never seem to get my bones warm. Depression covered me like a wet quilt.

Unlike me, when James could no longer bear to live in our world he made the decision to opt out of our life. Every minute of every day he was overwhelmed with constant reminders of his fractured family. He blamed himself. God forgive me, but there were times when I so wanted to opt out too. The deep down, rock solid pain of loss I felt when Kevin died was a knife that punctured my every cell every minute of every day. It was so intense that I would have done almost anything to stop hurting. But I didn't kill myself like James did.

Did I want to die? Every now and then, I did. I had never thought about hastening death along, but there were certainly moments when I didn't care about living. I so wanted to escape the misery and dark despair that walked with me, slept with me, ate with me every minute.

Since I had taken the option to die off the table, in time I decided it would be prudent to consider other options. If I could figure out how to escape the things reminding me of the recent tragedies, then maybe the pain I carried would ease somewhat. If I could do that, then there was a chance for me to find my way out of the deep hole of depression stuck to the walls of my soul.

I needed to get away from Bear River Falls to a place where there were no obligations, no reason to do anything at all that required more energy from me than blinking. I begged the God I was no longer sure I still believed in to guide me to a place where I could go and NOT have to think or remember, a place where my battered heart could begin to heal.

During that raw, awful time I had the safe place I'd made for myself in the attic before James died. It had been good for me when my broken heart was healing from the tragic loss of my youngest son but after James died, that space no longer worked for me. It served only to remind me of death. What I required at that time was some place to go and be completely away from all the things connected to sadness.

Did I want to leave Jake at that time? Oh no. I hated going away from him, but I knew if I ever hoped to maintain even a shred of sanity, I had no choice but to leave him behind. On some level, I was certain that if the two of us that were left were to come out of the dungeon that chained both our souls, then it would be necessary for me to escape to somewhere safe so I could pull myself together. I was, after all, the boy's only surviving parent. I was the adult.

Fortunately, or maybe not so fortunately, Jake was dealing with his own demons in his own teenage way. His feelings were of great consequence to him but not at all similar to my own. To be honest, I felt that Jake no longer needed me. Being around him during that span of time seemed to cause us both more pain than not. I was there, but I was not really there. What I represented to Jake at that time was what was left of his formally intact family.

That concept was not one the boy knew how to handle appropriately. How could he have known? Jake had traditionally circumvented our issues and when he continued to do just that, I figured it was just his way and there was not a whole lot I could do about it. He refused to talk to me about anything and that only added to my misery. In my mind, I was more alone than I had ever been in my life.

So there you have the reason I left home. I found out later that I was criticized all over town for leaving my child, the one who didn't seem to give a damn whether I was there or not. Funny thing though, I didn't much care what others thought nor did I care what they said. I knew what I had to do in order to become a whole person again and to be a good parent to the one child I had left. So that is what I did.

Lavonia, bless her heart, agreed to live in the house again and to look after my son for the entire time I was away.

"Aynnie, you go on and do what you gotta do. Me and Jake? We'll be just fine, so I don't want you worrying 'bout that. Stay as long as you need to. What you been through ain't gon' get healed overnight."

She was right. It took a very long time for me to become whole again.

In my next letter, which I hope I have made easy for you to locate, you will find a memento from the time when I went away from Bear River Falls to heal my broken heart and shattered soul. I will tell you in the letter where I went, how long I stayed and how I managed to find myself again.

Love from Aynnie

Cassie

At long last I have a window into what Jake's long held resentment for his mother is all about. It might even be the reason he holds back from telling me much of anything about his parents. I can't help but notice the antagonism he seems to feel about Aynnie, however, and now that I've come to know her, I have been even more puzzled by his attitude.

What teenage boy, having just lost his father could possibly understand adult pain or needs? That kind of insight only comes to a person after the boy within matures and lives as an adult. The ability to feel the kind of conflicts and sorrow that grownups sleep with each and every night is something one must grow into and learn how to deal with.

Oh Jake. There's so much I have learned from your mother, yet still so much I need you to share with me. I love you more than you can know and I feel the ache in your heart, although right now there is no way you can be aware of it.

CHAPTER 27

Dear Jake's Bride,

What you are holding in your hand is a Native American Amulet Bag traditionally worn to keep evil spirits away. This particular one, you may already have noticed, has a different design on each side. One side was inspired by the colorful blankets woven by Native Americans and the other draws its inspiration from the season of Spring: flowers, birds and a restful green. You've already discovered how I feel about spring, right?

Amulet bags were also used to house special items. What I have placed inside this one is a semi-precious Peridot given to me by a wonderful Native American woman who befriended me when my life was at ground zero.

"This, my sister, will help to remove your stress and heartache," Woya told me. "It will guide and protect you on your journey."

"My journey? What does that mean," I asked her.

She smiled and said, "The journey you are now taking to find yourself again."

I was skeptical. If her piece of rock could show me how to crawl out from under my own rock of depression, then fine and dandy. If not, I would look around for something that could.

"Tell me more about the Peridot stone, Woya," I said.

(Before I forget to mention it, Woya's name is a Cherokee word for "dove" and as you must be aware, the dove has always been a symbol of peace. As soon as I learned about that, I began to seriously think a higher power just might be working in my behalf.

Woya graced me with another one of her enchanting smiles. "Oh, Aynnie, the Peridot is a wonderful stone of lightness and it counters the effects of negativity. It balances emotional releases and brings them to comfortable levels of security and inner peace. It lightens suffering and will even help you sleep. The Peridot is very powerful."

Those words meant everything to me, especially the possibility that this stone, as improbable as it sounded to me at the time, might even tackle my insomnia. I had not slept through the night for months because of all the dark thoughts occupying my mind. Lately, those thoughts threatened to dig in and stay put forever.

Woya told me that the Peridot would take my burdens, guilt and obsessions and replace them with new clarity and feelings of wellbeing. I tried to make a joke by telling her that we should sell the Peridot stones to pharmaceutical companies and get rich quick, but my meager attempt at humor were lacking my normal Joie de vivre, so my joke fell flatter than pita bread.

In time, I was to learn that holding onto the past was the thing holding me back and was counter productive to my being able to achieve the wholeness I was searching for. Having the Peridot stone with me at all times, believe it or not, reminded me to detach myself from outside influences as it guided me toward a higher energy when I needed it. It also helped me throughout my journey to understand that I had a spiritual purpose. It sharpened my mind and showed me how to be open to new levels of awareness.

It sounds very new age and woo-woo now as I write about it, but for the first time ever, I became intimately close to the Me living inside my soul. Label it if you wish; it doesn't really matter now. All that does matter is that it worked to bring me back to my world.

I was angry and confused when I showed up at Rekindling Retreat in the Western North Carolina Mountains. I was told that Anger at God is not uncommon after experiencing devastating losses like mine. Woya said that the Peridot stone would calm my nervous system as well as the raging anger I had been unable to shake.

Life there was simple but fulfilling. Simple is an understatement; it was downright primitive. We heated with wood and our water came from a spring down the mountain—ten times better than bottled water, believe me. There was no television, of course and cell phones at that time were still in their infancy so I didn't own one, and I still don't. The retreat often made me feel like I was smack dab in the middle of an Amish community, simple beyond anything I had ever experienced. What a perfect environment to resurge my overburdened soul.

The emphasis the guides placed on my personal journey, as well as the love and support I was given never wavered. Not once. Two months went by before I felt strong enough to face the world I had abandoned. With the enduring help of my Native American friends, I was confident that whatever the future held, I could handle it. When I learned to acknowledge my weaknesses I found a way to tap into my inner strengths.

Looking back over the years since that time, I can honestly say that I have been able to handle whatever obstacles attempted to block my path. When I was diagnosed with Leukemia, it was enough to knock me down again but it didn't and it still doesn't. Because of the Rekindling Retreat, I am dealing with my illness hopefully with grace, and I'm even able to look to the future.

This project, this memory trunk that you and I have embarked upon, is proof positive of my faith in the future, whatever it turns out to be.

"Not creating delusions is enlightenment." — Bodhidharma

Love from Aynnie

Cassie

I had not realized that keeping my secret from Jake would weigh so heavily on my heart until I finally downloaded at least a part of it. I woke up a few mornings after our heart-to-heart talk and told myself that it was now time to make Vichyssoise out of what felt like the fifty-pound sack of potatoes I had been carrying. It had gone on for much too long.

Jake was still sleeping like a puppy with a full tummy when I got out of bed, so I went to the kitchen and made coffee. It was Saturday and if he took care of all the little chores around the house that I told him needed his special touch, I would need to postpone going upstairs to the attic until after the weekend. If I could talk to Jake over the weekend about my secret life with Aynnie, then the next time I went up to the attic it would be with a clear conscience.

No doubt I was itching to climb those 14 steps again, but that itch would have to wait until Monday to get scratched.

***

So now it is Monday morning and Jake is leaving for Banner Elk to take a deposition.

"I'll be gone all day, Cassie," he tells me while getting dressed. "If things get dicey, I may have to stay overnight but I'll call and let you know. Cross your fingers that won't happen."

He gives me a long kiss goodbye and I can't help but feel that it is more meaningful, less perfunctory than our goodbye kiss had been the previous Friday morning. Communication is truly the magic that makes relationships pop.

The dirty laundry is spinning away in the washing machine when I take the 14 steps to the attic for my next visit with Aynnie. Miss Priss, fully invested by this time as part and parcel of our attic adventures, bounds up the steps ahead of me.

I so wish I could talk to Aynnie in person, face-to-face. I would be so happy to tell her that her son had finally broken his silence about Kevin. Alas, I will just have to be content believing that her spirit has been next to me throughout, and that maybe—just maybe—there is some way for her to be aware that good things are happening to those she loves.

Digging into the trunk, my hands fall on top of a large envelope. I open it to find a post card in a plain black frame. In it there is a picture of a sunrise on Mount Pisgah located along the North Carolina Blue Ridge. As always, a letter of explanation from Aynnie is there.

CHAPTER 28

Hello Darkness, My old Friend ~Simon and Garfunkel

Dear Jake's Bride,

I love this picture postcard. Not only does it bring back memories of the Rekindling Retreat, the rising sun reminds me that each day I am given another shot at life. Bought while I was in residence there, when I came back home I had it framed. I placed it on my dresser so that I could look at it and be reminded of all the life lessons I had learned.

It was not easy to return home to a son with an attitude. Jake was furious at me for having left and it was easy to understand his anger. He was just a boy but he had lost two important people in his life. When I took off to the retreat, I became number three.

If I had allowed myself to get bogged down in hindsight, I'd have questioned whether I had done the right thing by leaving. I had total confidence in Lavonia and none in myself, so it wasn't hard to convince myself that Jake was better off without me. Until I could pull myself out of the blackness that swallowed me every moment, I felt I was no good for him or myself.

Little did I know the enormous amount of resentment Jake had built up. Had I not been so absorbed in my own anguish, I might have seen how going away, even with the promise of returning, made him feel abandoned. Leaving Jake to fend for himself emotionally will forever be my cross to bear. Jake had always kept his thoughts and feelings to himself, but he let me have it when I came back home to Bear River Falls from the retreat. The effects of his fury are still burned on my brain and heart and will haunt me for all my days.

"Why did you even bother to come back," he demanded. "It should be obvious that I can get along just fine without you. Maybe better. Go on back to wherever you ran off to and get yourself pampered some more. I don't need you."

I tried to explain.

"Jake, I had to get away from the sadness. Surely you can understand that. Everywhere I turned I saw Kevin and your daddy. It got so bad that I couldn't even think straight, couldn't make decisions, couldn't sleep and convinced myself that I was no good for you or anyone else. I hated myself. I had to go away and get my head together because I couldn't do it here, not surrounded by all the memories. Please try to understand. It was about me, never about you."

He smirked. He stood right there in front of me and smirked. "It's always about you," he said as if speaking to a hated adversary. "When was the last time you ever gave a good goddamn about me or anybody else?"

With that, he stormed out of the house. I don't know where he went but he didn't come home until late the next day by which time I was frantic. Thank God Lavonia was still with me.

She saw what was happening and put her arms around me while I cried. I thought my tears would never stop. Before that day I figured I couldn't manufacture any more tears but I was wrong. Both of my children possessed the power to break my heart and both of them did.

I can hear Lavonia's sweet voice even today. "Aynnie, you had to do what you had to do if you was ever to come back to being yoself. Nothing wrong with that, you hear me? Had you stayed here in this house with all the sorrow it holds, Lord knows what would have happened to you. Wasn't hard for a body to see you was not in any shape to mother that boy of yours."

I knew she was right but what was done was something I was never unable to undo.

"Lavonia," I said, "I've lost over half of my family and more than half of my soul. I can't lose Jake, too. He's all I have left."

She gave me one of her magnificent smiles. "He'll come around, Aynnie. But like you had to go off so you could find out how to deal with all this stuff, he got to find his way, too. And he got to do it by hisself. He's a good boy with a good head on his shoulders. Don't you worry too much about him because he's gonna work it out and then y'all will both be okay."

It was a mighty long time before we were even halfway okay again. While we were getting there, I made it a point to pick up the framed picture on my dresser each morning and gaze at the sun rising over the mountains I so loved. Then I would say a prayer that Jake and I would find a way to get beyond our splintered relationship. I prayed for the light illuminating the world to shine down on my son so that he might see his way clear to forgive me for whatever he thought I had done. And every day, I would then go downstairs with renewed hope that we would get right with each other. Most days, however, my son looked at me as though I were a slug. If I dared to speak to him, he responded in one or two-syllable words, always spoken in such a hateful voice that my heart broke all over again.

Like the song goes, we got to walk that lonesome valley by ourselves.
Love from Aynnie

Cassie

Do not stand at my grave and weep. I am not there, I do not sleep.
I am the swift, uplifting rush of quiet birds in circled flight. ~Mary
Elizabeth Frye

I replace the letter in the envelope and the sunrise photo as well. Then I put them both back in the trunk and close the lid. For a few minutes, I am unable to move from the spot on the floor where I have been sitting for the past hour or so.

Jake's surly side that Aynnie described in her letter is foreign to me and hard to imagine the sweet, considerate man I love being so rude to his mother. Granted, he was a teenager, young and confused about a great many things. But still.

Aynnie's latest letter feels like goodbye. It's just a feeling I have and I'm not sure what to make of it. There is so much I need to think about and even more I need to understand.

I gently pick up the cat from my lap and put her on the cold floor. "C'mon, Miss Priss. Mommy's got to clear her head and the only way to do it is by taking a long run and an even longer soak in a hot bath. In that order."

The cat, because she's the most brilliant feline ever born, reads my mind. She shoots down the 14 steps to wait at the bottom for me, tail thumping impatiently and demanding as only a cat can do, that I get cracking and give her a treat, which of course I do. Was there a choice?

I change into sweats and Nike's, do a few stretches and then take off running. It is an overcast day. Heavy clouds looking a whole lot like water balloons spread across the sky. I figure I will get soaked, but so what?

Any fool knows that running in the mountains is not the easiest thing to do because of the hills, but my house is not far from a small cemetery built on a piece of flat land. I head in that direction. Five circles around the cemetery is equal to a little over a mile, but given my need to exhaust my mind of a bunch of stuff, I go around it fifteen times. Whew! That promised long soak in the bathtub is going to feel mighty good.

There are a bunch of walkers who come to the cemetery early each morning and a few more like me, who enjoy running around the perimeter later in the day. Some even bring their leashed dogs to run along with them. Haven't seen any cats yet and I seriously doubt I ever will. Miss Priss agrees. She shows no interest in abdicating her princess status and certainly not her throne.

By the time I get to the cemetery, the geriatric brigade has already walked the one-mile they do each day and gone on back home to knit or whatever they do until time for Wheel of Fortune and Jeopardy!

Since marrying Jake and moving to Bear River Falls, I have made a habit of running at the cemetery but I've never stopped to visit Aynnie's grave. Today, I feel a need to do just that—actually, more than a need.

I know where Aynnie is buried because Jake and I have left flowers there on Mother's Day and Christmas, so I wander over there because, as opposed to the other days when I knew nothing about Aynnie, I am going there today to visit a friend.

Once I am at the site, I stoop down, pull a few weeds from around her tombstone and then try to straighten up the silk flower arrangement that the wind has taken for a ride.

"Well, hey, Aynnie. It's me, Cassie."

CHAPTER 29

Cassie

I am amazed at how peaceful it is here. Well, not so amazing when I think I am surrounded by dead people. When I plop down on the ground next to my mother-in-law, the damp grass feels nice on my butt. I am exhausted from running and grateful no one else is around.

"I read the letter you wrote, the one with the picture postcard from the time you spent up in the mountains. I might be one of the few people who can fully understand the need to get off by yourself in order to think things through. I suppose that's why I am here today."

I squirm a little bit and then brush some ants off my right leg, not wanting to kill them because it seems redundant to kill things in a cemetery, even ants. As it happens, the ants and I are the only living entities hanging out in this acre of ground today.

Now that I'm here, I'm not sure what I want to say to Aynnie. Up to this point, she has been the talker, while I have been the listener, occasional commenter or reader as the case may be. I've absorbed her words and many times have wept into the wedding handkerchief because of them, combining my tears with hers. Should I tell her? Is that why I am here sitting on the hard ground swatting ants and getting my behind soaked on the too-tall grass?

"Hey, Aynnie, the thing is I have a problem, kind of. It's not a huge one, but it's one that doesn't want to let go of me. It's about Jake. To me, he is the sweetest, kindest man I have ever met, so I'm having a tough time connecting the boy you described in your last letter with the man I married. I don't know the kid with all that adolescent anger. He has never shown that side to me."

Just as I finish the sentence, spoken out loud as if I were talking to my NBFF across the table at Starbucks, a female cardinal flies over my head and lights on the monument next to where Aynnie is buried. The bird looks directly at me, so I look right back at her. She just sits there on her newfound perch and stares. After a bit, I pull my eyes away.

"So Aynnie," I continue to converse with Jake's dead mother. "This is the thing: since Jake has been so secretive about you, Kevin and even his dad, I'm thinking it is all about unresolved grief and unhappiness. And if that is the case, then it's time for him to get it out of his system once and for all. If not, I'm afraid it will come out at an inappropriate time.

"What am I doing, Aynnie? Am I borrowing trouble like Momma said when I was worried about something that hadn't yet happened? Probably."

I think I must be sitting on a damn anthill. The freaky little critters are rushing around all over the place. It's an army of ants and they are all soldiered up and ready to sting me to death right here in the cemetery. How appropriate. I stand up quickly and brush them off my legs and shake them from my shoes while looking around for another place to sit or squat. People should put benches at a gravesite instead of headstones. They would get a ton more visitors.

"Aynnie, I'm just trying to figure things out and there's nobody to ask. Apparently Jake has chosen silence instead of talking about his family, so that puts him out as a candidate. I really want to be the best wife I can be to your son. I love him so much. But that unsettled side that I sense in him scares me because I don't know what to expect, not now or in the future. Should I take the initiative and tell him all the things I've learned from reading your letters? If I do, should I hope that it would make him finally open up about the part of his life he is still hiding? Or should I bide my time and wait until he decides it is safe enough to confide in me? Oh, Aynnie, I so wish you hadn't died. If only you were here now and we could talk about this face-to-face."

I stand back and read the words engraved on Aynnie's tombstone. Name, date of birth, date of death. And then, as I have done before when Jake and I would come to this place together, I read the inscription below her vitals.

There came a time when the risk to remain tight in the bud
was more painful than the risk it took to blossom. ~Anaïs Nin

Right in front of me is the answer I needed and asked for. I glance over at the cardinal that is still perched on the other tombstone and still staring a hole straight through me. I don't know what prompts me to do it, but while I am looking that bird in the eye, I say out loud, "Okay bird. I know you want me to think that you are Aynnie in bird form. I get it. But you should know that I do NOT believe you, so you should go now. You have my permission to fly away."

The bird doesn't move. She fluffs her wings a little bit instead and then moves her tiny feet on the top of the tombstone that has become her newest perch.

"Okay! Okay! You win. I read the tombstone message and yes! I promise to take the risk. I will tell Jake everything that's been going on over the past weeks and I'll do it tonight."

I look away from the bird and gaze at Aynnie's last resting place.

"There's one more thing I need to say to you, Aynnie. I want to tell you how much it means to me to have gotten to know and love you. You have made my life richer by far than it ever was before we met. That said, I believe the time has come for us to say our goodbyes. I won't be going through your trunk any longer because I don't need to. Your letters have given me the strength I needed. You get it, don't you?"

As though scared shitless of the crazy woman talking to dead people as well as winged creatures, the bird takes off.

I smile at Aynnie's remains. "I thought so."

I am too tired to run another step, so I amble out of the cemetery lost in thought. I hope to have everything that's been weighing so heavily on my mind resolved by the time I get home.

I turn the corner, knowing that the Anaïs Nin quote engraved on Aynnie's tombstone is significant. It was important for me to read it and comprehend the message.

At that moment an approaching car hits me and the next thing I see is blackness.

CHAPTER 30

Cassie

When I open my eyes I am flanked by people I don't know. I have no idea where I am or how I got here. Someone covers my body with a lightweight blanket. A paramedic leans over me.

"Hi there, Sleeping Beauty. Glad to see you decided to wake up. How are you feeling?"

I am not Sleeping Beauty and he is definitely not a prince. What I am is totally confused. What he is, well I'm too confused to figure out.

"I don't feel too good. Um ... am I having a bad dream?"

He smiles. Good teeth and deep dimples. Maybe he is a prince. I am flat on my back on the ground surrounded by a bunch of gawkers while a dimpled paramedic hovers over me. I have no memory of why I am here or why he is here, and yet I still have the temerity to take note of his smile? I have seriously injured my brain.

"No," he says. "You're not having a dream. You have been in an accident and we are going to take you to the hospital now. Okay?"

"I don't remember anything," I tell him. "What kind of accident?"

He smiles again showing off those dimples. "You were hit by a car and you may have a concussion from when your head hit the pavement. If that's the case, temporary amnesia is normal with head injuries. Don't worry, it'll come back before too long." He checks the oxygen tube someone had placed in my nose and says, "You ready to take a little ride on my four-wheel white horse, Princess?"

I nod my head. At least I think I nodded it. Maybe I just blinked my eyes.

"Excuse me," I say to Deep Dimples as I am being lifted onto a gurney. "My husband is at the office. I want him to meet us at the hospital. Can you call and tell him what's happened?"

"We sure can. What's his name?"

I give him Jake's name and somehow manage the correct phone number. Deep Dimples picks up his cell and dials. "Would you like to speak to him," he asks. I shake my head, which makes it hurts so much it feels like it's been used for soccer practice in the nearby schoolyard.

Apparently, I lose consciousness at that point because the next time I open my eyes I am lying in bed in a sterile hospital room hooked up to oxygen and an IV, hopefully painkillers. Might be Kool-aid for all I know. When I gingerly turn my head to the side, there is my Jake wearing an incredibly concerned expression on his face.

"Hey," I say to my husband. "May I have this dance?"

His breath catches and his eyes immediately fill with tears. "Oh, Cassie. Thank God you're conscious. I've been going out of my mind. How are you feeling?"

I have to think about it for a moment. There is a dull ache behind my eyes that hurts worse when I look toward the light. My entire head throbs, but it doesn't seem to be as bad as it was when I woke up on the street. I feel woozy, pretty drunk actually, so it probably has something to do with that Kool-aid bag dripping stuff into my arm. News flash! The stuff is not entirely working.

"Ouch! Everything hurts. Jake, I don't know what happened. The EMT guy said a car ran over me but I don't remember even seeing a car, let along getting hit by one. I am positive I didn't see one. Do you know who was driving?"

He sighs, gets up, walks over to the window and stares out. "Apparently, the driver didn't see you either. The man who hit you was old Mr. Tom Langston." Jake shakes his head. "That old fool should have had his drivers license revoked ten years ago. He's got to be close to ninety-years-old. God. When I think ..."

"Mr. Tom hit me with his car? Oh, that poor man. He must be devastated. Jake, I hope you spoke with him and assured him that he's not to feel bad about this. It was my fault. If I hadn't been preoccupied, if I'd been paying attention to my surroundings it wouldn't have happened. No way it was that sweet Mr. Tom's fault."

Jake looks at me like there is severe brain damage going on, which I have to admit scares me a little. "Mr. Tom is in jail and that is exactly where he belongs, Cassie. Damned old fool. He was probably half-asleep at the wheel."

I stare at Jake for a moment before thinking I must have heard him wrong.

"Tell me you're not serious, Jake. Mr. Tom wouldn't hurt a fly and if you have pressed charges against him because of what happened, you just better do whatever it is you have to do to uncharge him. You said he is in jail? Oh my God, Jake. It could kill the man."

Jake's face is flushed, a sign of anger I have seldom seen. "You could have been killed, Cassie. As it is, you are suffering from a concussion, a broken leg, three broken ribs and very possibly you will need minor plastic surgery to repair that gash on your forehead. What would you have me do? Tell him it's perfectly okay that he ran over my wife and put her in the hospital? I assure you that is not going to happen."

I have a broken leg? Shit. Broken ribs? No wonder my body feels like an oversized root. In addition, there is another thing I am all too aware of and that is an overwhelming weariness. I am way too tired to argue with Jake but the idea of that dear man, my sweet new friend, cooling his heels in a jail cell makes me want to scream.

"Jake, I am the victim here, not you. I don't need you to be my lawyer because I have no intention of pressing charges against Mr. Tom. Now listen to me and carefully because I'm not going to repeat myself. I want you to go right this minute and get that sweet man out of jail. And Jake? If you don't, you can be sure of one thing: I will never speak to you again."

CHAPTER 31

Cassie

My hospital stay is brief. I am there for only two days. My head feels as though I've been stoned, but nothing can be done about broken ribs except to suffer in silence. The cast on my leg is more complicated. I am now the proud owner of a compound fracture of the tibia and fibula, which means I can't put weight on that leg at all for a while. I left the hospital yesterday wearing an unfashionable ten-pound plaster cast while holding onto a pair of crutches and a shitty attitude.

After everything that happened when I left the cemetery, I decide I need to take one more trip up to the attic. I assure Jake that I'll be just fine on my own and tell him to go to work because he's getting on my last nerve. I almost push him out the door.

I manage to hobble up to the second floor but the attic is on the third. I am pretty sure I can climb those 14 steps before I'm old enough for Social Security, but the question is: will I be able to get back down again without breaking my other leg? It's been three days since I connected with Aynnie and told her goodbye, and as crazy as it sounds, I miss her. I also feel I owe her some kind of explanation. Yes, I know how crazy that sounds.

Standing by the attic door debating whether or not to attempt the climb, I realize not for the first time how much of a presence Jake's mother has become in my life. When I was sliding her in between household responsibilities, meetings, shopping or whatever, it was easy to think of the experience as a lark. A few days without her, however, has awakened me to the fact that she is more than a trunk full of letters and memorabilia. She is a part of me now and that thought makes me grin all over myself.

It looks like I will be stuck lugging this damn cast around for a good while yet, so what the heck. I might as well take my chances with the 14 steps. If I can't make it back down again, then I'll just wait until Jake comes home so I can yell for him to come rescue me.

"Miss Priss," I call to my cat. "Come on. We're going to visit Aynnie so we can give her the proper goodbye she has earned and richly deserves."

I take the stairs ever so slowly but the cat runs on ahead of me, thank goodness. Miss Priss has been sniffing my cast and wondering what it is all about since I came home from the hospital. Nosy, nosy, nosy. The last thing I need while making my way up the 14 steps is for her to suddenly decide to use my cast for a scratching post.

I bless myself for thinking to leave pillows on the floor next to the trunk. Squatting down while maneuvering a leg cast is not the easiest thing to do and I am grateful that nobody can see the awkward and horribly unladylike position in which I accomplish the task.

Today as I reach down into the trunk, I have to dig deep in order to pick up what I think is the next letter and when I do I am surprised to find that it is the only item left that I haven't opened. How had I not seen that before now? The only thing I can think is that I was so into the last letter Aynnie wrote that nothing else caught my attention. Now that I have told her goodbye, it seems appropriate that I think of her last letter as her goodbye to me.

There are no accidents is an expression I have hear all of my life, and while I have not always subscribed to that notion, the thought of no accidents gives me pause today. What if what happened to me was fate? What if old Mr. Tom is destined to play a major part in my big picture? What if I was supposed to meet him in the library and he was supposed to run over me with his car? Lord have mercy. I sound like a Presbyterian.

The instant my fingers touch Aynnie's final letter, I am convinced that she placed it on the very bottom on purpose in order for me to find it on my final visit.

My fingers are trembling when I put the box with the attached letter in my lap, take the letter out of the provided envelope and begin to read.

CHAPTER 32

Aynnie

My dear daughter-in-law,

I saved this one until now for a good reason. What you will find when you open the attached white box is what I trust will be a lasting memory of our attic adventure. At this point, I am still alive and kicking and I don't know diddlysquat about the hereafter. But what I hope is that my spirit has accompanied you up the 14 steep steps and remained with you each time you opened the lid to the trunk. I wish I could tell you that it is a certainty, but we both know that is the one secret none of us can be sure of while we're plugged into the earth.

That said, I want you to know that I will bust my butt once I get to wherever I'm going to make sure I walk up those steps with you in spirit and that I will remain with you until one day when we embrace each other in heaven.

Meanwhile, please keep what I've left for you in this box in such a place that you will be reminded of how much you are loved, even by someone you never met.

With love, as always from Aynnie

Cassie

The box contains a full-color photo of Aynnie as an older woman, probably taken before she was diagnosed with Leukemia. It has been matted and framed beautifully but it does not compare to the loveliness of the woman herself.

I know immediately that I will place this picture of Aynnie on top of the dresser in our bedroom downstairs, and that I will start out each day looking at the woman who loved me enough to make me a part of her family even though we never met.

CHAPTER 33

Cassie

I butt-walk back down the stairs and am surprised at how easy it is and at how quickly I get back down. Jake comes home from the office a bit earlier than I expected him to and although I figure it is because he thinks I'm an invalid, I am happy to see him. Last night, maybe because of the accident and my feeling so rotten, plus my discomfort from a leg cast I'm pretty sure weighs three hundred pounds, we seemed to distance ourselves from each other. I hardly slept and I doubt he got much sleep either.

The distance seems to have grown in part since I told him about my visits to the attic and my newfound relationship with his dead mother. I thought it was only my imagination, but after a few days I became convinced that Jake thought I needed long-term therapy.

How surprised am I when he walks into the house holding a huge bouquet of daisies, my favorite flower. I burst into a big smile and immediately the smile erupts into a giggle.

"What's up with this? Did I do something right for a change or something wrong as usual?"

"Neither. I simply felt like bringing my crippled up best girl a bunch of flowers," he says.

I grin so big I think my face might crack. "Did you hear me complaining? Nay, nay kind sir. I so love that you remembered how much I love Shasta daises. Just wondering what prompted the surprise is all."

"Come with me," he says and helps maneuver my clunky self into the den and over to the built-in bar. He pours himself a hefty slug of Jack Daniels and then turns to me. "Shall I pour you a glass of wine?"

I nod, hobble over to my designated chair and wait. Whatever he's got up his sleeve should be interesting.

"I've been doing some soul searching," he says after we clink glasses. "And in so doing, my unconscious has demanded that I bring up a lot of stuff to be closely examined. It's stuff I've managed to avoid thinking about for years, Cassie. Looking at it now has not been easy."

I resist the urge to hobble back over and wrap my arms around this dear man, this husband of mine who is and always will be the love of my life. I want to 'there, there' him to death while assuring him that everything will be okay. But I don't. I shut my mouth and get ready to listen to whatever he's got on his mind.

He clears his throat. "When you told me about your little trips up to the attic, that was one thing. But when you said you were engaged in some kind of weird relationship with my mother, dead now for several years, to be honest I thought you might be having a meltdown. I mean, even you have to admit the whole thing is pretty crazy, right?"

I nod. "Jake, that's the reason I kept it from you for so long. I knew you would think I was nuts but I'm not. I didn't want you to stop me from going up there."

This time he nods. "I realize that now, Cass. But at first, I was scared. Really scared. Whether you can understand it or not, you became my whole life when I fell in love with you. If anything like that ever happened to you I don't know what I'd do."

He drains his glass and then turns to refill it. I watch him for a minute or so before turning my gaze toward the softly glowing fire in the grate, so glad that I remembered to get it going before he came home. It was not easy dragging that three hundred pound cast, but looking at it now I realized I didn't do a half-bad job. I've always been told that an open fire tends to make people open up. I hope Jake does that tonight.

Before turning back to face me he says, "I thought my mother was a little bit crazy so when you told me about what all you discovered in the attic, including her rants and ravings, my first thought was No, no, no. Not again!"

He turns to me then. "I know you are okay but you can see why I was so afraid, can't you? I was scared to death for you and for us. Especially after finding out that you had learned all of the uh, family history—the good, bad and things better left under the rug."

"Oh, Jake. Your mother wasn't crazy. She lost herself for a while having to deal with so much heartache but I admire the way she dealt with one tragedy after another. It was enough to make most people go crazy, but she managed it without pills or booze. In my opinion, she did a good job of handling those horrible events in her life. She had to find a way back to herself and I hope you are learning to appreciate how difficult that had to have been for her."

He stares me down. "You didn't grow up with her, Cassie. You have no idea."

I am struck by his sudden outburst and my need to defend Aynnie. Crazy? No, she was never that. Maybe she went about things in ways that other folks might consider abnormal, but Aynnie McMinns was as sound as a dollar used to be. I will bet my last one on that.

"Jake, all kids, especially teenagers want to trade their parents in for a brand new set. That is the most normal thing in the world. Your mother handled things differently than some other people might have, but most people don't have to deal with the deaths of two family members back to back. She wasn't crazy."

I thought about the gorilla story Aynnie had written about. "She was creative and fun, Jake. But most importantly, she loved you with every cell in her body and don't you ever forget it."

He scoffs. "Well, that's debatable."

I shake my head. "No, that is one thing that is not debatable. I hope when you're ready, you will take the time to read all the letters she left because so many of them are about you. Too many of them are about her inability to reach you when she felt you needed her the most."

He takes a sip of his drink, sighs and gazes at the fire.

"She never told me that she had a twin sister, so it blew my mind to find out that she had been kidnapped when they were little girls. Why wouldn't she have told me that, Cassie?"

I have to think about it. "Maybe it hurt her too much to talk about it. Maybe by voicing it aloud, she feared it would put the onus on you. I don't know the answer, Jake, and she never gave a reason for it in any of her letters. When you think about it, though, it's really not a story most mothers would choose to tell a child.

His head turns quickly to face me. "Children do grow up. She could have told me about it later. God, if I had known don't you think I might have considered a career in criminal law? Who knows, maybe I could have used advances like DNA to find out exactly what happened to her sister. Instead, she chose to shut me out of that part of her life, a part that might have helped me to understand her better."

I put my wine glass down, get up from the wing chair and hobble over to where Jake is staring into the fire. Coming up behind him I put my arms around his waist. "She is telling you now, my love. She's telling you everything through me because it was the only way she knew how to do it."

His gaze remains fixed on the fire. "She told you about Daddy, too. About how he died? That was not for me, Cassie. That was for you. I never wanted to remember that my father ended his own life. I still don't want to acknowledge it. It is too horrible."

"Jake, it is what it is, or was. It's long past the time when you need to acknowledge what happened back then so that you ... so that *we* can go forward."

When I look up at him there are tears rolling down his face. He turns around and folds me in his arms. "Easier said than done, Cassie."

I pat his back and hug him while pretending I have not noticed the tears.

"You're right, Jake. But now you have me to help you. I'm here and I'm not going anywhere. You don't have to tackle it by yourself. Besides, all of the family skeletons are out of the closet now, so there's no longer any need to be afraid."

It is a breakthrough. Acknowledging some, if not all of his past is a start. It is not the entire answer, but even a small start means going in the right direction. I know we will get through whatever lies ahead for us, especially when it comes to dealing with the family secrets as I now think of them. I realize it will take time, but time is something we both have plenty of.

CHAPTER 34

Cassie

I am amazed that I can manage to drive myself down to the Food Pantry to volunteer this week. Because of the accident, I was forced to take some time off from preparing and distributing food for people who have no place else to go. Somehow I move clumsily around the kitchen with this cast dragging along behind me like an unwanted third cousin.

I love my volunteer work here among the homeless families, so many of them with children. The parents come to us because they have no money with which to buy food. It reminds me of the research I did at the library about the Great Depression and its impact on North Carolina. Little did I realize at the time that Bear River Falls would be battling similar issues.

A bittersweet feeling comes over me each time I work at the Pantry. I am happy that we can provide for those who come to us, but it makes me so sad to look at them and see the hopelessness and sense of failure etched on their faces. As if any of it were their fault.

Today as I wrap a ham sandwich in foil (best for later) and pack chips and juice in a box, I look up from my busyness to see a woman I haven't seen here before. She looks back at me. I think maybe I recognize her from somewhere other than the Pantry, but then I figure she must be a newbie, bless her heart. The woman looks around as though she doesn't know how our system works or what she is supposed to do. Her face, like many others who come through our doors, is haunted, an expression that most of the recipients here seem to have in common.

I silently thank the good lord that even after my parents were killed, I had people who cared enough about me to take me in and love me. I am so grateful for that and for Jake who is determined to take care of me now and to share my life no matter what.

If looking after these people, so down on their luck, has any significance for any of us, it must be a way to awaken our sleeping humanity. I have been volunteering here for over a year and the people we serve have grown to an enormous number over the past ten or so months. I am reminded of Aynnie's grandfather during the Depression and his noble efforts to do whatever he could for those in need.

I reach out and touch the woman's arm. "Would you like a sandwich, dear?"

She smiles. It is a sad smile, but at least she makes an effort. Good for her.

"Yes, I would," she says quietly. "Thank you very much."

I hand her the box lunch I just finished making up and she thanks me again before turning away. I watch her leave by the front door and find myself hoping she will turn back around and gift me with another one of her smiles. She does not.

Before long, I am busy wrapping more sandwiches and then cleaning up the mess I always make. Still, the woman's face and slight smile haunts me. She is only one of the many people who find themselves in dire straits and it breaks my heart to think how it must pain them all to have to ask strangers for a sandwich.

The woman, and in fact some of the others that we fed this day, weighs heavily on my mind even as I am on my way home. Home, my safe place, my refuge. I don't know why this day has seemed harder on my soul than any of the other days spent at the Food Pantry, but it doesn't want to let go of me. I resist the urge to call Jake as much as I would love to talk with him about it. He was in court all morning so I won't disturb him. He'll probably play office catch-until early evening.

If Jillie were here, the two of us would sit down over a bottle of wine and she would let me spill my guts and then we would cry together and ask God why the hell bad things have to happen to good people.

But Jillie is in Georgia and meanwhile Jake has become my surrogate BFF. Jake has gone through a lot himself lately, so I know without a doubt that when I tell him about my day he will be empathic. My sad feeling will find the human connection I need.

CHAPTER 35

Cassie

The minute Jake's large frame comes through the back door, the look on his face says he intends to head straight to the bar for a slug of Jack.

I want so much to tell him about my day at the Food Pantry, about the woman I met and how she has remained on my mind. What I don't want him to do is halfway listen to me because of other things he has on his mind. I have no idea why I can't forget about the woman today, but I just can't. It was something about the way she looked at me and something about her that made me want to know her better.

I follow him into the den, hobble up behind him and put my arms around his waist. "Bad day, darlin'? You look like you might have looked forward to that bottle of Jack more than you did me."

He shakes his head. "We lost the case I've worked on for months and I am so pissed about the verdict. I thought it was a shoo-in." He swallows the whiskey in one gulp. "I can't understand how it happened."

I pour myself a glass of wine and suggest we sit down by the fire and talk it over. We do. I sit. He slumps. I feel so bad for him because I know how hard he worked preparing for trial and although he has lost cases in the past, this one was special to him.

His client, a young girl who was thrown from a moving vehicle when it went out of control, is paralyzed. Jake's firm was suing the car manufacturer for a malfunctioning airbag. She was wearing a seatbelt but it came loose on impact. What was even worse was that the airbag did not deploy as it was supposed to. She was hurled through the windshield and thrown out of the car onto the hard surface of an interstate highway. The girl was eighteen-years-old.

"Life is so Goddamn unfair, Cassie." He looks like he wants to cry. "The one good thing to come out of this is that I will appeal until justice is served no matter how long it takes. I'll go to the Supreme Court if I have to. That girl doesn't deserve to be in a wheelchair for the rest of her life."

I wait a moment for him to say something more. He doesn't. "It sounds like we both had a day full of feeling, Jake. I 've been depressed ever since I left the Food Pantry."

He looks up from his drink as though seeing me for the first time. "Did something happen? Gosh, I've been so self-absorbed that I forgot to ask you about your day, Cassie. Tell me about it. It'll get my mind off the seething anger growing in my head like a cancer."

I tell him about a little girl clinging to her mother's skirt, about how she was too shy to look me in the eye. "She was no more than a waif, Jake. Skin and bones. Lord only knows when she last had a hot meal."

Jake gazes at me while I run through my day of feeding the hungry. I finish up by telling him about the new lady with the haunted smile, but by that time his mind is far away from my conversation. I keep talking so he can continue to feign interest and hopefully it will get his mind off the trial.

The same idea goes for me. I need to talk about the thing that sticks in my brain like a cancer, the pervading human condition that breaks my heart once a week when I volunteer at the food pantry.

"There's something else, Jake, something I really need to tell you."

His head jerks up at this and I realize he's afraid of hearing more bizarre tales from the McMinns attic crypt. His expression makes me laugh.

"You look terrified, husband of mine. What must you be thinking?"

He laughs, too, and the awkward moment is quickly diffused.

"Jake, what I need to say is that I think it's time for us to start our family."

There! I said it.

Well, that was probably the last thing he expected me to come up with and if I thought his former expression was laughable, it doesn't come close to the one gazing back at me now.

He continues to stare but still doesn't say a word. I don't either. Finally he breaks the silence with, "When did you decide this? I thought the subject of babies was closed and locked up tight for at least a few more years. What's going on, Cassie?"

"Nothing is going on, Jake. I love you and I want to bring your child into the world. I think it's time for us to have our own family. You'll make such a good daddy and judging from the way you love to read instructions, why you can teach me how to be a good mother."

I grin with the hope of wiping the fear off his face that has quickly replaced the puzzled look of only moments before.

"Jake, you do want us to have children, don't you?"

He gets up, walks over to the bar and pours himself another drink. My heart slips down to the bottom of my left foot. When he turns around, he says, "When I look at you, at your lovely face and think about the beautiful soul that lives inside of you, I don't want one more little Cassie. I want a house full of you. I have hoped for so long to have this conversation and I thought it might never come. I didn't think you wanted children."

Well, by the time he has uttered his last word, I'm a total mess. Tears do not trickle down my face; they burst out of my eyes and turn into a replica of Niagra Falls.

Jake comes to me, picks up my wine glass and says, "Drink up, Cassie my sweet, and come on upstairs with me. We need to get started making us a little Cassie."

CHAPTER 36

Cassie

The next night Jake apologizes to me for the knee-jerk reaction he had with regard to Mr. Tom when I was in the hospital. Sorry doesn't begin to cover his embarrassment when he finally thought about his rash behavior toward the old man.

"Cassie, I was so upset and so angry that you had been hit by a car driven by an old man I thought should have turned in his driver's license. I acted impulsively and I am so sorry."

"It's not me that needs an apology, Jake. I'm not the one who was thrown in the pokey."

He gets up from his chair and stokes the dwindling fire. "Cassie, I love old Mr. Tom. God. I've known that man all of my life. He was Daddy's client and he's my client today. Hell. He taught me in high school and he used to come over here to visit."

"I know. He told me your entire history the day I met him in the library. He even bragged that your dad represented him in all three of his divorces. He seemed rather proud of the fact that he managed to hook three wives."

Jake adds a new log to the fire and then stokes it pretty hard as if he's trying to hurt it. My guess is he's had another stressful day and needs to stab something.

"Jake, as I've said before, the accident was more my fault than Mr. Tom's. If I had been paying attention to my surroundings instead of wool gathering, I'd have heard the car coming up behind me and I'd have moved to the side of the road. I was walking on that big curve when I got hit, you know. And thankfully, Mr. Tom was not driving fast."

"He broke down and cried when I went to the jail to get him out, Cassie. And he kept telling me how sorry he was for causing the accident. Over and over. I assured him that he was not at fault and that we were not going to press charges."

When Jake turns around I look at his face and see how distressed he still feels for having caused Mr. Tom the indignity of jail time.

"So what else did you do, Jake? I hope you apologized to him."

He nods. "Profusely. Knowing him, however, he will philosophize the experience. Hell, he'll probably be holding lectures at the library before the week is out. "

"I hope it does. I'll be the first to sign up. I'm glad you apologized to him and now it's my turn to do the same thing. I want to invite Mr. Tom over for dinner and I promised him an invitation the day we met at the library. He said he was most interested in the restoration of the house since he was familiar with the original. Apparently, he was a close friend of your mother's and had visited here many times. So how about it? Are you good with that?"

He looks at me like I've swapped my brains for Miss Priss's kitty litter.

"And just how do you plan to entertain guests while you're bumping around in that less than fashionable and decidedly clunky cast? It takes you forever just to get to the bathroom from the kitchen."

I smile as if he is the one with kitty litter brains. "That's why I keep you around, big boy."

We laugh and then I tell him the secret I've been waiting for the right moment to share.

"Jillie is coming to see us. She'll be here day after tomorrow and she can help me cook and serve. I'm pretty sure she will fall head over heals for Mr. Tom, and all I've got to say about that is, God help him."

CHAPTER 37

Cassie

Jillie gives me a bear hug that lasts for a long time and even then it is not long enough. We both cry as realization hits us that we have allowed too much time to pass between hugs.

"Good Gawdawmighty, Cassie," she starts. "If you think I'm going out in public with you looking like you just lost a scrimmage game with Tom Brady, then you better think again sweetheart. Not gonna happen."

I lean in for another hug. "Do hush up. You will chauffeur me all over town and even to Asheville if I want you to, and you'll love every minute of it. Right now, however, I just want you to stop hugging me so I can hobble to the bathroom. I drank four cups of coffee waiting on you to get your tardy butt up here and I'm fixing to bust my bladder."

She rolls her eyes and then gives me one of her incredible smiles that can literally light up a room. "Oh all right, if you insist. But as soon as you are finished in there, I do believe it will be my turn. I have, after all been on the road for nearly six hours. When we're both done in there, it will be way past time for a tall Bloody Mary."

I stop short. "Jillie! It's only ten o'clock in the morning."

She gives me an impatient stare. "Ten o'clock? OMG. We are way behind schedule. Get your ass up so we can go to the loo, girlfriend. While you're in there doing whatever, I'll mix us up a pitcher of that wonderful red-as-blood elixir. Where do you keep the vodka?"

Jillie is on her third Bloody Mary when I tell her about Mr. Tom and how Jake threw the poor man in jail after my accident.

"OMG, Cassie. Did you go and marry yourself a Republican or what? I never heard anything so heartless in my life. And here I thought the man was your knight in shining armor."

Jillie was born a Yellow Dog Democrat and will die as one, no matter what. If someone gives her the stink eye, she rolls her own eyes and says, "Republican." If someone accidentally runs over a dog, she says, "Republican." She will never change and I hope she doesn't. Her passion is one of the most lovable things about her, even if I don't always agree with her.

I giggle. "Jake was just scared, Jillie, and he reacted like a man who has just witnessed his wife unconscious for the first time. Fortunately, Mr. Tom's jail term was short-lived. I told Jake if he didn't get his butt down to the clinker and get that old man out of there, I would never speak to him again. I meant it, too. If I had been able to think it through I'd have told him to get acquainted with celibacy."

It is Jillie's turn to laugh. "You know of course, had Jake been married to me, he'd have been more than happy to take you up on the 'I'll never speak to you again' option."

I look over at my friend, my non-blood sister and tears spring to my eyes unbidden. I love her so much. She is one of the best people I know and kind doesn't begin to cover her many attributes. I have not asked her, but I know in my heart that she dropped important things in order to be up here with me now. Why? Because I said I needed her.

"Well, this is the thing, Jillie. I want to invite Mr. Tom to come over for dinner while you're here. He's a thrice-divorced nonagenarian who lives alone. He reads Spinoza and Neizche for heaven's sake. Oh, and he taught Jake in high school and was also a close friend of Jake's family back in the day."

She gives me a puzzled look. "What is a nonagenarian? Is it contagious?"

"Oh gawd. I have almost forgotten how dense you can be. Mr. Tom is ninety-something."

The one Bloody I am sipping begins to kick in and I sigh. Mixing alcohol and painkillers is probably not the best course of action, but hell. It's not everyday my almost-sister is sitting with me in my very own home.

"You will love this guy, Jillie. And get this: he looks just like Clarence Oddbody."

She gives me another blank look. "Who the hell is that?"

"Clarence! The angel in *It's a Wonderful Life*. Remember how we used to watch that movie every Christmas Eve? You loved Clarence. We both did."

The blank look remains in place. "What kind of meds did you say you're on, Cassie? Pills and booze will make you form words that nobody can understand, you know. I'll drink your share of what's left of the Bloodies." She giggles.

I grin at the thought that in this very moment Jillie and Cassie are sitting here teasing each other just like old times. Can it get any better than this I ask myself?

"Okay. So how about it? Will you help me make a nice dinner for Mr. Tom? Something simple. Jake can throw steaks on the grill if we ask him to and between us, putting together the rest of the meal will be easy-peezy. Old people don't eat much I'm told."

Jillie rolls her eyes. "You can't prove that by what Momma shoves down her throat. She eats like the starving children in India or China she used to guilt trip us with. You remember her saying the children didn't sass their parents and they ate every bite of food on their plates, don't you? And do you think that skinny-ass broad would gain a pound with all she eats? She doesn't have to because I do it for her. I can look at freakin' sugar-free Jello and gain five pounds. Seriously."

We laugh because we're both just a tiny bit tipsy and way happy because we are together.

"When do you plan to get the old fart over here," she asks. "Do I have time to get to Dillard's for a makeover before then? I might want to be wife number four."

I shake my head, not in a negative way, but because Jillie is such a hoot. I wish I had her lively personality.

"How about Saturday night? Would that give us time to shoot over to Biltmore Village and stock up on all the new cosmetics? I need to feel pretty again."

"Saturday is fine with me. Hey, let's tell him to bring us some bootleg whiskey. I hear North Carolina is famous for two things: bootleg and giggle weed, that parsley looking stuff folks grow in their back yards way up in them thar hills."

CHAPTER 38

Cassie

I am hobbling around the table trying to get it set for dinner when I look out the window and see Mr. Tom as he runs over my azalea bush with his car. He gets out, leans over the seat to fetch an enormous bouquet of spring flowers. Then he reaches back inside for a gift-wrapped box of something. I yell for Jillie to go to the door and let him in.

"I'm too busy," she yells. "You go."

Jake is in the back yard cleaning the grill and I have no idea what Jillie's busyness is all about, so I ditch the place settings and fine crystal and managed to hobble to the front door by the time Mr. Tom reaches the top porch step.

Smiling about as much as a person can, he says, "Hello there, beautiful lady. Didn't your Momma ever tell you to beware of geeks bearing gifts?"

I laugh. "Is that what you are, Mr. Tom? A geek? You could have fooled me."

He steps onto the porch, armed with flowers and gifts. "I am indeed a geek, milady. At my age, one must choose between being a dinosaur or a hip old man. I might be old but I'm not ready to embrace a prehistoric label."

He hands me the flowers. I thank him and sniff the roses in the bouquet as we walk back into the house.

"Mr. Tom, you are so thoughtful and I think you must be a bit psychic as well. There was not one thing blooming in the yard for our dinner table tonight. This is perfect."

When we reach the den, Jillie pops out from around the corner.

"Hi there," she says all bright-eyed and bushy-tailed. "I'm Jillie, Cassie's best friend and almost sister. My real name Janelle but I read somewhere that people with names ending in ie are lucky in life. So I ditched Janelle to become known to God and everybody else as Jillie. Still waiting around on the luck to make an appearance, though."

Mr. Tom looks at my dippy friend as though she has announced the fact that she recently revised the Magna Carta. His eyes never leave hers. I, on the other hand, feel as though I'm about to introduce him to Miss Looney Toons.

"Tom Langston, meet my fruitcake friend, my wonderful sister, Jillie Scott. Jillie, this is the delightful man I told you about, the one who insists on bumping into me anytime we are within spittin' distance of each other."

I shouldn't have said that. Mr. Tom's face looks stricken by my words.

"Oh, my dear lady. I cannot apologize enough for ... for everything. Jake is right you know. I shouldn't be driving a car at my age. And now seeing you with your leg all covered in that dreadful cast, well I feel even more terrible."

I want to comfort him, to say it's okay, but before I can open my mouth, Jillie jumps in.

"Are you kidding? She's being pampered like a princess and is milking every minute of it. I have to cook for her and everything. Mr. Tom, I hate to cook. What you did was put Cassie on easy street, but poor little Jillie has to wait on her hand and foot. Thanks a lot, Buster."

Bless her heart. She has the ability to put even the most uptight person at ease. And that is just what she did. We are all laughing by the time Jake comes in from the backyard holding greasy hands up in the air.

"Hey, Mr. Tom. Ya'll go on in the den and make yourselves at home. Soon as he gets washed up, the resident bartender will be at your service." He looks at the old man and says, "I've got a bottle of 10-year-old single malt just begging for the two of us to sip on it. Laphroaig. Are you familiar with it?'

Mr. Tom shakes his head. "No, Jake. Not with that particular label, but I hope you know I will be more than happy to sip with you. I look forward to meeting Mr. Laphroaig."

Jake reminds the old man of former times while his dad was alive and good Scotch was enjoyed between client and attorney and even later when Jake became his attorney. He disappears down the hall toward the powder room. "I'll make you gals a martini when I get back," he calls over his shoulder.

Mr. Tom clears his throat. "Meanwhile, dear lady, if you would be so kind as to uncork this wine I brought for our dinner. It might need to breathe since it doesn't have a strange name. I'm told it is very tasty."

The evening proceeds with lively conversation, Jake's perfectly prepared steaks and two bottles of the lovely wine Mr. Tom brought.

"Shall we continue this discussion in the den," I ask. "Jillie and I will be serving a delicious apple pie made by that gourmet guru, the incomparable Mrs. Smith. It came straight from the coldest freezer known to Ingles and will be brought to you straight out of the oven. The coffee, I can assure you is tried and true and a sure bet. Trust me on that."

Jake rolls his eyes. "Just so you know, anytime someone says 'Trust me,' I get a creepy feeling, but if you put vanilla ice cream on that pie, my lips are sealed."

While Jillie and I are in the kitchen giggling over having to serve a store bought pie that would make both our mothers "Roll Over Beethoven" in their graves, Jake pours brandy for Mr. Tom and himself. His voice is low when he speaks to the old man, but I can hear every word.

"Mr. Tom, I want to apologize again for losing my cool after the accident. It was inexcusable and I can't tell you how bad I feel. I hope you can forgive me."

"Jake," the old man replies, "I'd have done the exact same thing so there is nothing to forgive. You were a man worried sick about your wife, as well you should have been. I am the one here begging your forgiveness."

Well, no way am I going to stand around, if you can call it standing, and listen to any more of this blame game they seem intent on playing. I limp into the den, leaving Jillie to dig hard ice cream out of the carton.

"Ahem," I say as I clump into the room. "There will be no more talk about the accident. None. Do you both hear me? Mr. Tom, it was not your fault, it was mine. I was distracted and not paying attention. I also had my iPod ear buds crammed in my ears with music playing much too loudly. As far as I'm concerned, it's over. The accident was then, and now is now. Let's all just forget about it. Okay?"

They both agree so I hobble back to the kitchen where Jillie is cussing like a sailor while hacking at ice cream with the largest butcher knife in my drawer. She turns to look at me, sees the incredulous expression on my face and says, "WHAT? I couldn't find a freakin' scoop."

We both burst out laughing. OMG, how I love that woman.

CHAPTER 39

Cassie

After two weeks of being pampered both daily and nightly, fussed at, teased unmercifully, hugged to pieces and having my spirits constantly refreshed, Jillie hugs me one more time, slaps me on the butt, gets into her car and heads home to St. Simons Island.

I spend the rest of the day alternately crying real tears for the almost sister I so wish lived next door instead of on the coast of Georgia. I laughed my ass off again and again while reliving the fun times we shared while she was here with me.

It was good that I had Jillie to wean me away from my attic addiction. The heavy cast on my leg helped a lot, too. The cast comes off next week and I will go back up to the attic and do some heavy cleaning out and getting rid of stuff. I know there are things up there that will go directly to the nearest charity but my guess is most of it will be things we'll choose to save.

I keep thinking about that small attic bedroom located off from the big room that looks more like a mini-sports arena. I seem to be drawn to the little room with the antique brass bed, the flowered wing chair and softly glowing lamp. The coziness of it even now when I think of it makes me want to kick off my shoes and snuggle up with a good book in there. It served as a getaway for Aynnie, so why not me?

How I wish Aynnie—the real flesh and blood Aynnie—was still around. Jake and I would turn that attic into a nice apartment for her and furnish it with the things she had loved. It would be all hers and she would have the freedom to come and go as she pleased, especially if we added an elevator to give her even more privacy. Oh, Aynnie. How I wish you had not left us when you did. It would have been wonderful to have more than just your spirit alive and well in this big old house.

It takes me longer to get dressed these days due to the cumbersome cast I still wear on my leg 24-7, but I will try not to bitch too much or too often. In a few more days I will see what's underneath that ugly piece of plaster, see if my leg has withered and died while I hobbled around. I have never had the patience of a gnat but these days I honestly feel that being forced to slow down has provided me with a measure of tolerance I was totally unfamiliar with in the past.

Hell's bells! Who am I kidding? I'm still as impatient as a hungry cat, especially one known in this household as Miss Priss.

Today it is my turn to volunteer again at the Food Pantry. It will be the second time I have been back to help since Jillie went back home. The people I work with there, as well as the folks who come in for food, have been so kind to me. One of the older women treats me like she's a borderline Momma hen and I'm her prodigal chick.

One of the clients is the same one that came in and I was so taken with her. I felt a connection to her then and I still do. There was something about her that made me want to hear her story from her own lips.

She told me that she has been homeless since her small house in South Carolina caught fire and burned to the ground. Her husband died in the fire and she was badly burned as well. Months in the hospital drained whatever money she had in the bank and left her penniless as well as homeless. She didn't appear to be resentful of the misfortune life had sent her way and she did not in any way dwell on it. In fact, I had to practically drag the story out of her.

She came to Bear River Falls because someone she met while in the hospital told her it might be a good place for her to start over. She hoped to find work, but she is in her seventies and no one seems to want to hire someone her age. Social Services is trying to find her a place to live so she can leave the shelter.

Why not offer her the attic, I think to myself. We're not using the space and it would be an enormous help for someone who had been through so much. I promise myself to talk it over with Jake tonight before I get too carried away. He may very well balk at the idea of a stranger living in our house and who could blame him? Lord! He just might start thinking I'm cracking up like he did a few weeks ago!

CHAPTER 40

"I love it when a plan comes together." ~ Col. John *"Hannibal"* Smith

Jake has come home early from the office and from the looks of things is happy to be winding down from an especially tough day in court. He walks into the house, kisses me on the cheek and heads directly to the den bar. Within seconds he has poured himself a splash of Jack.

A deep sigh emanates from somewhere deep in his soul. That sound only comes from him when he is relishing the protection he feels inside his personal fortress.

He sits in his recliner, picks up the newspaper and settles down to relax by the fire.

No sooner has he begun to look relaxed, however, than the doorbell rings. I tell him I'll answer it but he stops me as I head for the door.

"I might as well get it, Cassie. It's probably the courier from Judge Spalding's office with copies of the judgments I requested this afternoon." He folds the newspaper, sighs loudly as though the last thing he wants to do is look at another piece of legal paper.

"Hello," she says after Jake unlocks and opens the front door. "My name is Ruth Lowell and I hope I'm not bothering you, but I am moving to Bear River Falls soon and well, I'm afraid I don't know many people here yet."

Jake stares at her but says nothing.

She keeps talking. "I don't know how to explain my being here but for some crazy reason I feel drawn to this house. I must have walked past it a dozen or so times since I first saw it, and I can't for the life of me figure out why that is. I decided today to just knock on your door and ask you to tell me a little bit of its history, something to help the puzzle pieces fit in my brain," She laughed. "Anything you can say will be a big help. As crazy as it sounds, I feel like I'm walking around remembering a dream I may have had."

She ducks her head, suddenly self-conscious. "Oh I'm so sorry. I see by the look on your face that you think this is inappropriate and you're right. You must also think I am completely off my rocker. I should not have come here and I do apologize. Believe me, I didn't mean any disrespect. Please forgive me."

When Jake steps back, she glances over his shoulder and sees me standing behind Jake. I haven't said a word but I find it incredible that Ruth Lowell is my sweet new woman from the shelter and that she has found her way to my home. I move to stand closer to my husband at the door and when I do, I notice that her eyes are filled with tears.

"It makes no sense to me at all, but do you think it's possible I might have visited here maybe when I was a young girl? I know it sounds crazy but everything looks so familiar. I'm rambling on like an old lady. Again, I apologize."

She turns to leave and that's when Jake takes a deep breath. Then he calls out to her. "Ruth, do the names Laynnie and Aynnie ring any bells for you?"

She turns slowly back around to face us. Her teary eyes are wide, her face suddenly void of color. Her mouth opens but no words come out of it.

Jake reaches for her hand. "Aynnie was my mother," he says, "and you look exactly like her."

—End—

*"There is a tide in the affairs of men.
Which taken at the flood, leads on to fortune;
Omitted, all the voyage of their life
Is bound in shallows and in miseries." ~ Shakespeare*

ABOUT THE AUTHOR

Cappy Hall Rearick, an award winning short story writer and syndicated humor columnist, is the author of twelve published books. Her first collection of columns, Simply Southern, and her first novel, The Road To Hell Is Seldom Seen, were both nominees for the Georgia Author of the Year Award.

Rearick holds membership in the National Society of Newspaper Columnists, Georgia Writers, South Carolina Writers, Atlanta Writers Club, Florida Writers, North Carolina Writers and Southeastern Writers Association.

She lives in North Carolina where she is a popular public speaker and is often invited to instruct seminars in Southern Fiction, humor, memoir and short story writing.

Contact her at:
www.simplysoutherncappy.com or by email at: cappyhall@gmail.com

Made in the USA
Columbia, SC
12 October 2017